THE BLACK CIRCLE

THE BLACK CIRCLE

PATRICK CARMAN

SCHOLASTIC INC.

NEW YORK TORONTO LONDON AUCKLAND SYDNEY
MEXICO CITY NEW DELHI HONG KONG BUENOS AIRES

Library of Congress Control Number: 2009921984

ISBN-13: 978-0-545-09063-6
ISBN-10: 0-545-09063-6

10 9 8 7 6 5 4 3 2 1   09 10 11 12 13

Book design and illustration by SJI Associates, Inc.

Library edition, August 2009

Printed in China

Scholastic US: 557 Broadway · New York, NY 10012
Scholastic Canada: 604 King Street West · Toronto, ON · M5V 1E1
Scholastic New Zealand Limited: Private Bag 94407 · Greenmount, Manukau 2141
Scholastic UK Ltd.: Euston House · 24 Eversholt Street · London NW1 1DB

For Rachel Griffiths,
Master of the Cahill Universe.
Thank you for helping me
discover Russia's treasures.

—PC

CHAPTER 1

Amy Cahill liked to be the first one up in the morning. But not if it was because someone was screaming outside her hotel-room door.

"Telegram for Mr. Cahill!"

The words were accompanied by a thunderous knocking. Amy bolted upright in a panic, a terrifying thought racing through her mind. *Madrigals!*

The yell came again.

"Message for you!"

Amy, her brother, Dan, and their au pair, Nellie, had fled to a different Cairo hotel in the night, afraid they might be attacked by the mysterious sect they knew so little about. *The Madrigals couldn't know where we are, could they?*

Dan rolled off the fuzzy gold couch he was sleeping on and landed on the floor with a thud.

"No, Irina! Not the Catfish Hunter!" he yelled. Amy sighed. Once again, her brother was locked in a dream in which their cousin Irina Spasky was shredding a beloved baseball card with her fingernails.

"Wake up, Dan. You're dreaming."

Amy had never felt so tired in her life, and her brother was, as usual, acting like an idiot.

"Telegram!"

The knock at the door came again.

"Dan! Get . . . the . . . door!"

Amy stuffed her face in a pillow and screamed. She was awake for good and she knew it. Peering past her pillow, she saw that Nellie was still totally dead to the world.

"Coming!" cried Amy. "Hold your horses!"

When she reached the door, she hesitated, a familiar fear gripping her insides. What if she let someone dangerous in?

Come on, Amy, get a grip.

Amy opened the door, her eyes settling on an Egyptian bellboy standing in the hall. He was shorter than she was by a mile, wearing a spiffy red uniform with gold buttons up the front that was at least two sizes too big. In his hands was a sealed envelope.

"For you, madam, from the desk. Someone has leaved it."

Amy took the envelope, and the bellboy stepped a tiny bit closer, beaming at her expectantly.

"I bring message from the desk," said the bellboy. "For you, madam."

His feet were halfway in and halfway out of the room, which made Amy nervous.

"Is there something else you have for me?" asked Amy.

"Someone has leaved it for you," he said, pointing at the envelope with a happy grin.

"Give him this," said Dan. "Then I can go back to sleep."

Dan's voice was muffled, and when Amy turned around, she saw that he was talking into the carpeted floor, too lazy to lift his head. He was holding up a five-pound Egyptian note, worth about one dollar.

Amy shut the door. Curiosity had killed any hope of going back to bed. The envelope had been addressed on an old-style typewriter that appeared to be missing the capital A. The underline was also randomly stuck on some of the letters.

She tore it open and sat on the couch, her face whitening as she scanned the note. Saladin meowed hungrily and raised his back, claws bared on the gold bedspread.

"Dan, you better get up here."

Dan didn't move, so she yelled.

"TELEGRAM FOR DAN!"

Dan lifted his head as if mustering the energy for a comeback, but Amy could tell her brother was still clawing his way out of dreamland. He stood up from the floor and dropped heavily onto the couch. Nellie was still curled up under the covers on one of the two beds in the room, the thin white cord of her iPod earbuds snaking out from under a pile of seven pillows covering her head.

"That girl could sleep through a demolition derby," said Dan.

"Dan! Listen!" Amy said, holding the telegram as she began to read. "'Cairo International Airport, locker number 328. 56-12-19. NRR.'"

"Sounds like a lame trap set by one of our competitors. Let's order room service and go back to bed."

"I don't think so," said Amy. She held out the message so Dan could examine it. What he found on the paper took his breath away.

Lazy Dan left the building and was replaced by Alarmed Dan.

"No one knows about this, not even Nellie."

"Grace knew," said Amy. "You, me, and Grace. Whoever sent this must have known Grace well enough to get this out of her."

Dan was still too dumbstruck to respond, but Amy knew what he was thinking. Just last year he'd brought his prized collection of bottle caps to Grace's mansion — everything from Dr. Pepper to vintage Coca-Cola — and all sixty-three caps in a super-cool old-school cigar box. Grace had given him a spade and told him he could bury it on the property if he wanted. He'd told Amy and Grace where the treasure was hidden, even how deep he'd buried the box, just in case he died unexpectedly, snowboarding or skydiving. As he said at the time, it paid to be safe with a bottle cap collection.

Dan looked at his sister, his green eyes brimming with hope.

"Do you think Grace is helping us again?"

Amy and Dan both used Grace's name as if their grandmother were still alive, and for a moment it felt like she was. Their beloved old Grace, who'd given her heirs a choice: a million dollars or one of 39 Clues leading to immense power. Amy still couldn't believe where the chase had led them in such a short time. They'd traversed four continents and been nearly killed more than once by their own relatives. If there was even a chance Grace Cahill was still offering help from the grave, Amy knew they had to follow the trail.

"Come on. We're getting out of here."

Ten minutes later, Dan and Amy made their way down to the bustling hotel lobby with nothing but a backpack between them. Dan had insisted on bringing his precious laptop, and Amy had grabbed Nellie's cell phone, just in case.

"I left Nellie a note saying we went looking for doughnuts. Let's just hope this doesn't take all morning. What we need right now is a way to the airport," said Amy.

"No worries, I got it covered."

Dan opened their backpack and removed a wad of money, stuffing the rumpled bills into his pocket. It didn't amount to much, about fifty American dollars' worth of Egyptian pound notes.

"Yo! Cabby! Yo!"

Dan held out a few bills and waited.

"We're not in New York," Amy hissed. "Try to act like you have a clue."

As if by magic, a black-and-white car with a monstrous luggage rack pulled up and skidded to a stop. An Egyptian man jumped out and waved Dan and Amy over.

"Come, come! I have nice car for you!"

Dan tossed Amy an I-told-you-so look and marched for the car. The cabdriver hopped out and opened the door, then quick as a rabbit, snatched the backpack from Dan and headed for the trunk.

"No thanks, amigo. I'll keep the bag on me if you don't mind."

The driver didn't seem to understand, so Dan grabbed the backpack, handed the cabby a ten-pound note, and dove into the backseat, commando style.

Amy turned bright red and stammered an apology. She had a feeling Dan was warming up for a long morning of humiliating his sister.

"We're in a hurry, my man," said Dan, confirming Amy's suspicions. "The airport, double time."

"Fast is middle name!" The man laughed, slamming the door just shy of Amy's foot and racing for the front seat.

"You see there, sis? Everything is fine. This guy is perfect. Just sit back and re-*laaaaaaah* — !"

The cab (and Dan) screamed into traffic, weaving and dodging like an amusement park ride gone haywire. Amy was tossed into Dan, then against the door, then back into Dan as they dodged honking buses and irate pedestrians. When they hit a slow patch, Amy caught sight of a big problem behind them. She turned to her brother, wide-eyed and worried.

"He does leave a little to be desired in the safety department, doesn't he? I'll ask him to take 'er down a notch."

"N-N-NO! Tell him to speed up! Speed up!"

Dan glanced past his sister's stricken face to the bright yellow Vespa zigzagging between cars behind them. Someone in a purple sweat suit was riding it, and that someone was huge.

"Hamilton Holt!"

It was Hamilton Holt of the Holt clan, a family of nitwits also in search of the 39 Clues. The last time Amy had seen him, Hamilton had left her for dead in a Tokyo train tunnel.

"Step on it!" yelled Amy, but the driver didn't seem to hear her. Dan pulled out another precious ten-pound note and tossed it into the front seat.

That seemed to get the driver's attention. His foot came down on the gas pedal like a hammer and the cab swerved violently into high gear. For the next ten minutes, Dan threw more and more money into the front seat until, at last, they looked back and Hamilton Holt was gone. When the cab lurched to a stop outside the Cairo airport, Dan checked his pockets. They were empty.

"Is okay," said the driver, grinning from ear to ear. "You pay plenty already!"

"Nicely done, dweeb. Now we're stuck at the airport with no money. Nellie's going to love us when we wake her up and she discovers we've stolen her phone, spent most of our cash, and need a ride from the airport. And we don't even have any doughnuts yet! Could it get any worse?"

"I think it just did," said Dan.

Amy's heart sank as a black stretch limo pulled up to the curb behind them, and a door opened.

Ian and Natalie Kabra, a Clue-hunting team infinitely more dangerous than the Holts, had arrived on the scene.

CHAPTER 2

Most of the time, Dan Cahill would rather show up to school in his underwear than get involved in his sister's love life. But this was different.

Ian Kabra emerged from the limousine with a smirk the size of Texas plastered on his face, as self-assured as ever. Dan glanced over at his sister. Amy was glaring at Ian, but Dan could see her hands were trembling. This guy—this *ogre*—had not only lied about liking his sister, he'd tried to trap them in a cave. And leave them there forever.

It was time to lower the boom.

"You've got a lot of nerve showing up here after you tried to *kill* us!" Dan shouted.

"Let's not get carried away. Your little brother has a big imagination," said Ian, taking a step toward Amy. "You know I'd never actually hurt you."

Dan knew if Amy tried to talk it would come out all stutters. He wasn't going to let Ian Kabra anywhere near his sister.

"Hold it together, Amy," he whispered.

"I'm *fine*," said Amy, but now her lip was quivering ever so slightly. Dan lashed out at Ian.

"Get back in your monstermobile and leave us alone!"

Ian gave Amy a sideways smile, then sauntered up to the cabdriver.

"Well done, my lead-footed friend. We had quite a time keeping up with you. Although I suppose it wouldn't have mattered."

"What's that supposed to mean?" asked Dan, eyeing the revolving doors into the airport terminal.

"You children play expensive games!" said the driver as he took a roll of rubber-banded bills from Ian and handed over a slick new phone in return.

"Espionage must have been so much harder before GPS, don't you think?" asked Ian.

Ian's sister, Natalie, emerged from the black limo like a model about to stroll down a media-frenzied red carpet.

"Did you sleep in those pathetic things you call clothes?"

Dan looked down at his zip-up hoodie, which was wrinkled beyond all imagining. Oops. He actually *had* slept in his clothes.

"Wrinkles are the new thing. Ask Jonah Wizard. He'll tell you."

"Make this easy on yourself and tell us why you're here," said Ian, moving closer to Dan and Amy. Amy's eyes were locked on Ian's face, like a mouse confronted by a cobra.

The cabdriver laughed at the scene playing out, got in his cab, and cranked it alive. A plume of black smoke burst from the tailpipe as he sped off, covering Natalie with a thin layer of soot. She howled and clutched protectively at her hair, which was just the diversion Dan needed.

"Come on, Amy!" he yelled. He grabbed Amy by the hand and bolted for the revolving doors, but Ian was quick on his feet and snatched Amy's other hand. Dan pulled one way, Ian pulled the other. People were starting to take notice of the ruckus.

"Let my sister go!" yelled Dan.

"I think she likes it when I hold her hand," said Ian. "Don't you, Amy?"

Amy didn't say a word. She reeled back and kicked Ian in the shin harder than she'd ever kicked anyone. There was a loud crack and Ian lost his grip, bouncing up and down on one leg as Dan and Amy ran for the revolving doors.

"Direct hit!" cried Dan.

"So long, suckers!" Amy yelled over her shoulder.

"Get them!" howled Ian, hobbling toward the terminal entrance with Natalie and their driver, a guy who looked like he could crack concrete with his forehead, close behind.

Once inside, Dan and Amy darted among a sea of people with rolling luggage, but the Kabras stayed on their tail.

"This way!" said Amy, taking Dan by the elbow and dragging him into a busy travelers' store filled with candy bars and magazines. Seconds later, they were out the other side and into another store, through a web of foreigners. Dan was sure they'd lost the Kabras, but when he peered carefully around a corner, he saw Ian limping toward them, staring into his phone.

"Uh-oh," said Dan. "I think we've been had."

Dan took off his backpack and started unzipping compartments. Hidden in the front pocket was another cell phone, the GPS blinking their position.

"Double-crossed times two!" said Dan. "That cabdriver must have planted it when he got ahold of my backpack at the hotel."

Amy looked around the corner once more. The Kabras were getting really close.

"Give it here," she said, taking the phone from her brother. "I know just what to do with Ian's precious gadget."

Amy moved back into the flow of oncoming people with Dan close behind. She swept quickly across the wide corridor and dropped the phone into a passing baby stroller, then ducked into a bookstore and opened the first book she could find. The stroller was attached to a mother who was clearly late for a flight, parting traffic as she ran for her gate.

The Kabras were so intent on watching the screen on Ian's phone that they walked right past Dan and Amy, then broke into a run themselves.

"Nice play!" said Dan. "I hope that kid drools all over their expensive technology before they get it back."

Amy shot Dan a triumphant smile. Clearly, out-smarting the Kabras—*especially* Ian—had put some Cahill sizzle back in her step.

"Let's find that locker," she said.

The locker wasn't very big, about one foot square. But it was plenty full. There were three items inside, which Amy removed one at a time.

"This looks like a paperweight, don't you think?" she asked, holding a honey-colored glass ball in the palm of her hand.

"Let me see," Dan said, reaching out to grab it.

"No way! Knowing you, it'll get dropped on the floor and smashed into a thousand pieces. Let me have a look first."

Dan didn't protest. He had already imagined what a marble that size would look like rolling down the long airport corridor.

"Try holding it in the light a little more," said Dan.

Amy squinted up at it. "It looks like a room, and there's a mother inside, sitting on a chair."

"How do you know it's a mother?" asked Dan.

"She's holding a baby, stupid."

Amy looked closer.

"There are three letters on one of the walls—TSV—and ew! I think that's an eye staring back at me from another wall."

"Creepy," said Dan.

Amy held out the glass paperweight and told Dan to put it carefully in the backpack for future investigation. He hated it when she treated him like a three-year-old, and the temptation to roll the honey-colored ball down the airport corridor returned. He held it in the light again instead.

"Did you see the key?" asked Dan.

"What key? What are you talking about?"

"On the bottom," said Dan, rolling the paperweight over. Under the floor of the room there was a small key hidden in the glass. "When the time comes, I get to bust it open."

"The paperweight was holding something down," said Amy, lifting out a thin piece of parchment about the width and length of her own hand. It was filled with ornately drawn letters, numbers, and lines.

"It looks like someone spent a lot of time misspelling words," said Dan. Something about the way the letters were grouped looked oddly familiar to Dan, but he couldn't pinpoint what. Especially with his stomach grumbling.

"Is there any food in that locker? I have *got* to get something to eat. Brain . . . needs . . . candy."

Amy ignored her brother and reached one last time into the small space. At the very back of the locker there was a ten-inch-square box.

"I hope it's full of Rice Krispies Treats," said Dan, yanking the box out of Amy's hands.

"Hey! Be careful with that."

Dan looked like he wanted to give Amy a wedgie, but she was quick to calm him down.

"Sorry, okay? I'm just nervous. Open it up."

Dan removed the lid, riffled through the contents, and then busted out laughing.

"Check me out! I'm a nineteen-year-old beatnik from San Francisco!"

Dan held out the first of two passports, expertly forged with Dan's name. The photo showed Dan with a goatee and mustache, along with John Lennon glasses.

"Let me see the other one," Amy said. Dan flipped open the second passport and nearly fell over.

"You really need to fire whoever's cutting your hair."

Amy grabbed the passport from Dan. In it, she was wearing a short black wig and stylish red-rimmed glasses.

"I'm twenty!"

Dan had already pulled out each of the parts to make his disguise and begun putting them on, setting Amy's wig and glasses aside as he went.

At the bottom of the box, under the wig, Amy spied an inch-thick paperback. Dan knew it was love at first sight.

"A Russian guidebook! And it's well worn, like someone already used it on a long trip," Amy exclaimed.

"Looks like dullsville to me."

"What if it's another guidebook Grace used?"

Dan knew better than to get his hopes up.

"Still dullsville."

But Amy was instantly captivated. It was her favorite kind of book: weathered so she didn't need to take special care of it, with a story of its own because it had been in the possession of who knew how many travelers before her. As she flipped through, she came upon two tickets tucked between the pages about a certain city.

"Two airline tickets for Volgograd, Russia, with our names on them," she said. Amy looked at her watch. "Leaving in one hour. Why would anyone think we're stupid enough just to hop on a plane to Russia?"

"Check this out!" said Dan. There was one more thing at the bottom of the box, and as far as Dan was concerned, it was the best item of all.

He held up a shiny new Visa gold card with his name on it.

"Peace, love, and a Visa card! YES! It's GOLD! Let's go get some doughnuts! Let's go get some video games! Let's go get some computers!"

"Calm down, Dan! You're scaring me."

Amy put on her dark wig and tucked in her natural reddish-brown hair. She stuck out her tongue. With the red glasses on, she was virtually unrecognizable.

"You look weird," said Dan.

"Speak for yourself." Amy laughed. "You've achieved total dweebdom in that getup."

"Thank you."

Dan had the piece of parchment in his hand and turned it over. His heart flipped. He looked up, no longer goofy and excited.

"Amy . . ."

"Dan? What is it?"

Amy reached for the parchment, but Dan instinctively pulled it close. This was a treasure he never intended to let go. He looked at his sister.

"We have to catch that plane."

CHAPTER 3

When Amy Cahill dreamed of traveling the world, she'd never pictured herself sitting next to a pint-sized John Lennon.

"I don't think we're going to find doughnuts in Russia," she muttered, staring at her brother's goofy round glasses.

"Not to worry! We're covered," Dan answered. He was staring into a bottomless pit of snacks. Their backpack was loaded down with candy bars and bags of chips, purchased by Dan with help from his new best friend, the Visa gold card. Dan opened a bag of Doritos and leaned back in his seat.

Amy was more focused on what they should be doing than stuffing her face with junk food. She'd finally convinced Dan to let her hold the parchment so he wouldn't cover it in Doritos dust, but staring at it only heightened her concern. The telegram they'd gotten that morning was from someone who called himself NRR, which meant nothing to Amy or Dan.

Worse was the fact that Nellie's phone was dead, so they couldn't reach her.

"Do you think we can trust NRR? I mean, we're on our own here. Nellie can't protect us this time. This whole thing could be an elaborate setup."

"All I know is four hours on a plane with this mustache is going to kill me. It itches like crazy."

"Can't you be serious for one minute? We're on our way to Russia. *Russia*, Dan. Do you get that? Without Nellie or Saladin."

Amy knew Dan loved Saladin and couldn't bear the idea of being away from him for very long. And no Nellie? She wasn't their mom, not even close, but she was a pretty good stand-in given the crazy situation they were in.

"Let me see that thing again," said Dan, snatching the note from Amy's fingers.

He held the parchment in his hand and looked at the scrambled letters, then he reverently turned it over. Amy knew it was the photo on that side that most intrigued him. She watched as he looked at it, his attention riveted on the black-and-white image of a couple, young and clearly in love, standing in front of the American embassy in Russia.

"It's really them, isn't it?" asked Dan.

"You bet it is," Amy answered.

In Paris, Dan had lost his only picture of their parents and Amy knew what having a new one meant to him. But it had also sent them both into a tailspin.

Mom, Dad, what were you doing in Russia?

Amy hesitated. "It's amazing seeing them like this, so young and happy. I mean, it's the perfect bait. How horrible would it be if someone was using this picture to manipulate us?"

"I get what you're saying," said Dan. He ran his finger along the edge of the photo, touched his mom's face, gazed into the eyes of a dad he could barely remember. "But if there's a chance to find something out . . ."

Amy knew how Dan felt because she felt exactly the same way.

There was a message in script below the picture, and Dan read it aloud for about the hundredth time, trying to make sense of it:

The clock is ticking. Find me in thirty six hours or the door to the room closes forever. Come alone, as your parents did, or don't come at all. Trust no one. NRR

Dan flipped over the parchment to look at the scrambled letters again. He stared at them all the way through takeoff while he munched through a second monster bag of Doritos. It wasn't until the beverage cart arrived and he guzzled an entire Coke that Amy could see things were starting to click.

"Where did you say we were flying to again? Volvoflurb?"

"Volgograd," Amy replied.

"Riiiiight. Give me that envelope the bellboy handed you this morning. I have an idea."

Amy was using the envelope as a bookmark. She pulled it out and gave it to Dan, curious about what he was up to.

"This should do it," said Dan. He ripped a page out of an in-flight magazine and pulled out a pen, writing down one of the word combinations.

RGOLGOVAD

"That was the problem, the missing letters. It was confusing me. But they come from the envelope — this one's VOLGOGRAD, see?"

Dan took the underlined L from the envelope into the mix and unscrambled all the letters. Amy flipped to a page in the guidebook listing cities in Russia, and a few minutes later Dan and Amy were staring at a list of six.

RGOLGOVAD	Volgograd
OCOSWM	Moscow
ENBIRGKRUYEAT	Yekaterinburg
GBSUXRTEPRETSZ	St. Petersburg x 2
DNAGABERSAMIAI	Magadan, Siberia
BAERMKSISOI	Omsk, Siberia

"Yekaterinburg," said Dan. "Sounds like a place where they throw up a lot. Can we skip that one?"

Amy didn't bother commenting. She had already figured out something else.

"We have a leftover X and a 2 with the St. Petersburg one," said Amy. "I bet that means X2. St. Petersburg, times two. It must mean there are two things we have to discover there."

Dan nodded. "Now we just have to figure out what we're supposed to do in all these places."

"Volgograd is where this plane is headed, so it has to be the first place we're supposed to search. It's also shown in this paperweight," said Amy.

"How do you figure?" asked Dan.

She held the heavy glass ball out where Dan could better see it.

"The letters on the wall—TSV—those stand for Tsaritsyn, Stalingrad, and Volgograd. According to the guidebook, they've renamed the city twice."

"The Russians can't make up their minds?" asked Dan.

Amy ignored her brother's question and leaned in closer. "I think I know what we're looking for once we land."

"You've been holding out on me!" said Dan, wiping his salty fingers on his goatee.

Amy tapped the cover of the book she'd found in the locker. "These things are full of answers. You just have to open one up once in a while."

When Dan saw Russia for the first time, he choked on a corn chip and coughed it up onto the airport sidewalk.

"Ew! Seriously, you will *never* have a girlfriend," said Amy.

"Like I'd want one!"

Dan considered a sneak attack on his sister, but just then all his senses fired. Every sign was a collection of strange and swirly letters, impossible to read. The air was thick with flavors yet to be tried, red-and-yellow buses lumbered by, and everywhere Dan heard the sound of a new, exotic language.

They glanced back and forth outside the Volgograd airport terminal looking at the jumbled lines of dirty taxicabs. Neither one of them was sure someone else could be trusted driving them, especially after the GPS snafu in Cairo.

"What about that guy?" Dan asked through a mouthful of Kit Kat. It was his third candy bar in as many hours, and his voice was coming out a little jittery.

"Don't let him catch your eye," said Amy. "He'll never leave us alone."

But it was too late. The driver was already blasting across four lanes toward them. Dan had a feeling about the bearded Russian with the Volkswagen van.

It suited his beatnik style to ride around in a vintage 1960s peacemobile.

"No worries. I speak this guy's language."

"Is wearing that mustache making you dumber or something?" Amy asked.

The van veered wildly across the road and skidded to a stop in front of Dan and Amy.

"We want to rent our own ride," said Dan. "Can you help us out?"

What?! Amy mouthed. *Rent a car? Who was going to drive it?*

"You want car of your own? I know guy. Best deal in Volgograd."

Dan had never driven a car, but he was pretty good on a dirt bike. He flashed the Visa gold card, then slid it back into his pocket.

"Can you get us a motorcycle? We like the open air."

The bearded Russian winked, and less than an hour later, Dan was pulling out of a back alley with Amy jammed into a sidecar beside him. It was a vintage Russian military bike, army green with a kick start.

"Are you sure you can handle this thing?" asked Amy, clutching her guidebook.

"Hold on! This is going to be a bumpy ride," said Dan. The grill of a delivery truck blasted by, then Dan veered out of the alley and gunned it.

"Slow down, you maniac!" Amy howled, but Dan was having the time of his life. It took him several tries to get out of first gear and the engine redlined. Horns honked and pedestrians glared as the bike swerved all over the road. Dan finally got ahold of second gear and headed into oncoming traffic, nearly letting go of the handlebars as the bike careened out of control.

"D-D-D-D-Da . . ." spluttered Amy, pointing to an oncoming slew of honking traffic. Dan slammed into third gear and raced back into his own lane.

"I'm really getting the hang of this," he yelled, zipping along in traffic with a grin as wide as a monster truck. Amy tore off her wig and red glasses, stowing them in the backpack.

"You're going to get us killed is more like it!"

"Don't worry about a thing. I got this!"

Amy pulled on a beat-up old helmet she'd found rolling around on the floor of the sidecar. Then she grabbed the guidebook and turned to the back page, where the bearded Russian had scribbled directions.

"We take the third left," she yelled, glancing up in search of directions. Every sign she saw was written in Russian, and they were just about to pass the turn they needed.

"Right here!" Amy screamed, white-knuckling the sidecar as Dan slammed on the brakes and swung the bike into a hard left.

"This is awesome!" howled Dan, leaving a black streak of burned rubber behind the bike. "Eat your heart out, Hamilton Holt!"

It was twenty hair-raising minutes until the bike came to a stop in a football-field-size parking lot.

Dan tore off his helmet, mustache, and goatee and gazed up over the sprawling grassy knoll. On the far end there stood a massive statue of a woman holding a sword over her head, rising like a skyscraper into the cloudy horizon. They'd seen it in the distance as they raced across the city, but up close it was a frightening spectacle.

"The Motherland Calls," said Amy. "It's twice as tall as the Statue of Liberty. Do you know what it commemorates?"

"Don't have a clue, but I'm sure you're going to tell me."

"The Battle of Stalingrad in World War Two, and it's nothing to make jokes about. Over a million people died right here."

Parents had died here, leaving children to grieve in the care of others. Dan knew how awful that felt. All the unanswered questions, the frustration, the terrible sense that you'd lost your place in the world. Amy reached for her jade necklace, the one from Grace, and rubbed the pendant.

"Better get the show on the road. Never know who might be following us," Dan said, starting up the pathway toward The Motherland Calls.

There were people everywhere—families, old couples with canes, sightseers galore, and uniformed guards.

"I was hoping we wouldn't run into anyone here," said Amy. "This place is crawling with police and tourists. Take it slow and easy, okay, Dan? Better safe than sorry."

Dan nodded and suggested they split up to cover more ground. Amy had figured out that the mother sitting in a chair in the little glass paperweight was a reference to the enormous statue. One of the walls in the tiny room also had an eye on it, and this is where things got a little scary. If Amy was right about this being a reference to one of the eyes on the face of The Motherland Calls, it would mean climbing all the way to the top of a statue that was almost as tall as a mountain.

Dan looked up. And up, and up. *How are we going to get up there? And what are we going to find?*

CHAPTER 4

Hamilton Holt was the first to hit the pavement, followed by his sisters, who tumbled out in big-time wrestling mode, beating the tar out of each other. The Holts had tracked Dan and Amy all the way from Cairo in search of Clues, hotwiring a 1970s Eastern European van the moment they touched down in Russia. Landing at the Volgograd airport, they'd had no idea where to turn next, but the Holts were nothing if not conspicuously American. The same Russian who had picked up Amy and Dan smelled money and moved in for the kill. It didn't take long to put two and two together. Ten minutes later, the Russian was a hundred dollars richer and the Holts knew right where to go.

Gazing up at The Motherland Calls, Hamilton could tell that he'd finally arrived in a foreign land that might actually appreciate his size and strength.

"Gather round, troops!" howled Eisenhower Holt, the kingpin of the sweat-suited band of Neanderthals.

"Hamilton, front and center!"

Hamilton, the biggest and brawniest of the three Holt kids, darted to within three inches of his father's face and screamed, "SIR, YES SIR!"

"Son, you've got protein-bar breath and you're spraying spit again. Get it under control!"

Hamilton's face fell. It was hard to scream those Ss without showering *someone*.

"Won't happen again, SIR!"

Eisenhower nodded in stern approval.

"You're on point. It's our most important task. Figure out what those nitwits are up to and report back. Drag 'em back to the van if you have to. Got your two-way?"

Hamilton pulled a two-way radio out of his pocket, hit the call button, and screamed into it.

"SIR, YES SIR!"

Eisenhower pulled out his own radio and screamed right back.

"GO GET 'EM, BOY!"

Hamilton bolted toward the towering statue, proud to be at the center of the action. He glanced back at his family. His younger sisters, Reagan and Madison, were already duct-taping a GPS under the sidecar on Dan's motorbike. They complained bitterly about being hungry, and then Madison punched Reagan in the shoulder, which seemed to make her feel a little better. Mary-Todd, their mom, was on surveillance in the van, keeping an eye out for other teams.

"Must eat!" bellowed Eisenhower. The last thing Hamilton heard was his dad yelling something about spying a food cart loaded down with Russian meat pies.

It didn't take Hamilton long to spot Amy lurking around the front of The Motherland Calls. She was running her fingers along the stone, peering carefully at every seam and corner.

What's that scrawny geek up to, and where's that stupid little brother of hers?

He turned and saw Dan approaching from the other side of the statue. One was standing thirty feet to his left, the other ten feet to his right, and he didn't know which one to go after. The thought of disappointing his dad, *again*, put him in a cold sweat.

"Hey, Hamilton!" yelled Dan. "Did you see me on that motorcycle? Better than that donkey you were riding in Cairo!"

"It was a Vespa, you moron! And come say that to my face!"

Then, with Hamilton looking on, Dan signaled his sister by turning his hand as if he needed a key.

Hey! Do they think I'm stupid?

"Looks like someone's got a key," yelled Hamilton, turning to Amy as his two-way radio went off.

"Get moving!" boomed Eisenhower. "We've got company!"

Hamilton, Amy, and Dan all swiveled toward the parking lot in unison. Ian and Natalie Kabra were pulling up in a white stretch limousine, almost as if they couldn't bother to be inconspicuous. Eisenhower Holt started peppering the limo with meat pies from a huge bag, taking a bite out of each one before letting it fly. From a distance, it looked as if Eisenhower was unpinning hand grenades and throwing them into a bunker.

"Your dad is a menace. You know that, right?" asked Dan. He'd moved within ten wary feet of Hamilton, motioning Amy to toss him the glass paperweight. Amy dug inside the backpack, but Hamilton took four big steps and cornered her.

"What's in the bag? Come on, fork it over!" said Hamilton, looming over Amy. He was just about to rip the backpack out of her hands when Amy said something that shocked him.

"The K-K-K-Kabras are closing in on us," said Amy. Hamilton could tell she was desperately trying to get her voice under control. "How many c-c-clues do you have?"

Hamilton stopped cold. "We've got plenty! More than you two losers, I'm sure."

"We have ten. You have ten?" said Dan, looking Hamilton straight in the eye. His sister shifted from foot to foot, eyeing both of them warily. Grace had taught Dan how to bluff like a Vegas poker player, and Hamilton didn't know what to think.

"You got *TEN*? No way you got ten!"

Dad is going to freak out if we're that behind! he thought.

Police were beginning to swarm the place, making sure the mischief breaking out in the parking lot didn't spill over into the park itself.

"You could be a hero, Hamilton," said Amy. "You want to come back with something useful, don't you?"

That one hit Hamilton right between the eyes. There was nothing he wanted more than to please Eisenhower Holt.

"What have you got in mind?" he asked, glaring down at them.

He waited, watching the two Cahills as they stared at each other like each could read the other's mind.

Finally, Dan nodded. "Let's get the show on the road before it's too late," he said. "This way!"

Dan led the three of them around to the back of The Motherland Calls. The base of the statue was about as wide as a skyscraper, and the whole way around, Hamilton wondered if he should clobber Dan and Amy and take the backpack.

Calm down! Let it play out! If they trick you, then you can clobber 'em!

"Can you radio your dad?" Amy asked. "Tell him you've almost got what we came for and to keep the Kabras away from The Motherland Calls."

Hamilton gave Amy a searching look, then pressed the button and yelled into the receiver.

"Holt here! Mission nearing success. Stay clear!"

"Roger that!"

Hamilton turned on Amy and Dan. "Now give me the goods."

Dan hesitated, then pointed to one of the stone slabs on The Motherland Calls. "Before you showed up to complicate things, I hit the jackpot," said Dan.

Hamilton took a closer look and saw the letters TSV carved into the stone above a small keyhole. Amy saw it, too. She smashed the glass paperweight against the stone pathway.

"Hey!" yelped Dan. "That was my job!"

"Got it!" said Amy. The key was free of its round prison, and before Hamilton's unbelieving eyes, she inserted it into the stone panel. Dan pushed hard against the secret door, but it didn't budge.

"Step aside, shrimp," said Hamilton. He shoved Dan out of the way and smashed his frame against the smooth stone. The panel gave easily, and the three of them dashed inside.

"Close the door behind you, big guy. We've got work to do," said Dan.

Hamilton almost shoved Dan to the ground, but he knew it wouldn't take much to injure the little jerk, and that might complicate things.

"This better be good," said Hamilton.

"Don't worry," said Dan. "It will be."

With the secret opening firmly shut, Dan was able to breathe a sigh of relief and take stock of his surroundings. It was magnificent inside The Motherland Calls; wide open all the way to the top, with a web of beams and support systems all through the middle. Light trickled in from minute cracks that lined every side of the structure. Dan felt like he'd entered the shadowy realm of a gargantuan spider.

"Where's Gandalf when you need him?" asked Dan.

"You're a weird kid, you know that?" said Hamilton.

Amy frowned at both of them. "We have to get to the top, where the eyes are," she said.

"Bring it on," said Hamilton, peering up into the beams for the best place to start. "This will be a piece of cake."

Dan had already begun climbing a service ladder that ran two stories up into The Motherland Calls, but Hamilton had a different idea. He went straight for a massive steel beam running up the middle of the statue, with giant rivets on each side.

"See you at the top, losers!"

By the time Dan and Amy reached the final rung of the ladder, Hamilton had scaled the steel beam like a lumberjack racing up a redwood. He was way ahead of them, disappearing into the faint light above.

"We have to get there first!" yelled Amy. "Come on!"

At the top of the ladder, Dan saw something. The crisscrossing beams were also designed as narrow catwalks. They were a foot wide and flat, and there was a cable running above them for holding on to. But there was no rail.

"They must clip into the cable for safety when they're working up here," said Dan. "We can do this!"

"A carabiner would have been nice," said Amy. Looking up reminded her of a long series of rope bridges in an old movie. One where everyone falls into a bottomless canyon.

Dan grabbed the cable and began walking, first slowly, then faster and faster as he gained confidence. He was standing at the other side of the statue, twenty-five feet higher in the air before he looked back. Amy hadn't moved, and Hamilton was still fifty feet above them, traveling up the middle of the statue.

"Come on, Amy! You can do it!"

Amy took a deep breath and stepped out onto the beam. She wobbled back and forth, then stopped, gripping the cable tighter.

"Keep moving, Dan! I'll make it. Just get there first!"

Dan hesitated, his head pivoting between Hamilton ahead and Amy behind him. *It could be Christmas before she reaches the top!* he thought.

"Get moving, Dan!" Amy yelled.

Dan took off like a monkey, arms and legs working in unison as he raced up another twenty-five feet. He turned at the other side and sped up even more. The switchback routine gave Dan an advantage over

Hamilton: It was much easier going up this way than climbing straight up the middle. As Dan crossed the center of the statue for the fourth time, he overtook his larger competitor, who was gasping for air after having climbed over a hundred vertical feet.

"Nice day for a stroll, wouldn't you say?" called Dan. He was also totally out of breath, but his path to the top was *way* easier than Hamilton's.

The two-way radio was going off like a dinner bell, Eisenhower Holt screaming about the Kabras and demanding to know why Hamilton had disappeared.

Dan was only three switchbacks from the head of The Motherland Calls when he looked back. He couldn't see Amy.

"Amy! Are you down there?"

Dan's voice echoed through the open air. No reply.

"Amy! Answer me! How far behind are you?"

"You don't have to yell. I'm right here."

"No way!" said Dan, a huge smile lighting up his face. Amy had quietly caught up! She was only two switchbacks behind Dan and quickly coming even with Hamilton Holt, who had stopped moving.

"Double no way!" Dan heard Hamilton mutter. Hamilton had clearly had enough of climbing up the center beam. Thin support rods ran twenty feet away from the beam and connected to the catwalks, and Hamilton grabbed one as Amy walked past. The radio was turning to static, and the calls for updates were garbled at best.

"Hurry, Dan!" said Amy.

Hamilton swung along the steel support rod, his feet dangling over a hundred and fifty feet of open air. It didn't take long for him to reach the catwalk and swing his massive frame up and over. The first thing he did when he got there was turn off the two-way radio.

Dan knew he had to hustle. He raced to the end of the final beam, where the cable ran straight into a ladder leading into the head of The Motherland Calls.

"I'm heading into the brain!" yelled Dan. "Wish me luck!"

At the top of the ladder, Dan found a platform big enough for several people to stand on. Two thick streams of light poured into the head from outside. It was eerie, as if Dan really were inside someone's head, digging around in the dust for a hidden memory.

"There!" whispered Dan. A small cylinder wrapped in paper and tied with twine was tucked into the corner of one of the eyes. On quick examination, Dan saw that the top of the rough paper was stenciled with three letters: ST. P.

St. Petersburg!

Dan jammed the object into his pocket for safekeeping.

"I'm coming up," said Amy, reaching the bottom of the ladder.

"How far back is he?" asked Dan, pulling his gasping sister onto the platform.

Amy looked down at the catwalks below. "He's moving pretty slowly. I'd say three or four minutes."

"Perfect. I've got an idea."

It was a full five minutes later before Hamilton arrived in the head of The Motherland Calls and flopped down in the center of the platform. His chest heaved in and out, and a giant ring of sweat surrounded his neck.

"Dude, you look like a fish out of water," said Dan. "Speaking of which . . ."

Dan dug around in the backpack. Among the smashed candy bars and bags of chips were a few cans of Coke. He pulled one out, popped the top, and fizz shot all over Hamilton.

"Oops," said Dan, but Hamilton didn't seem to care. He sat up and guzzled the whole can, then tossed the empty over the edge. They all listened as the can pinged and echoed all the way to the bottom.

"We're way, way up here," said Amy, her face draining of color as it seemed to dawn on her for the first time that they'd have to get back down.

"I found a lead," said Dan, putting his plan into action. "And not only that, I *solved* it."

Hamilton perked up.

"Lemme see," he said, wiping the sweat from his brow with a swipe of his arm.

Dan pulled out the piece of parchment they'd gotten from the locker, the one with the scrambled words of all the places they were to visit. Dan had figured out, all on his own, that thirty-six hours wouldn't be anywhere near enough time to visit all the places on the list, and they only had twenty-nine hours left. He didn't want to admit it, but they needed help.

Amy seemed to get what he was doing. "It's a list of places, see," said Amy to Hamilton, taking the parchment from Dan. She was careful not to turn it over and reveal the picture of her parents or the note from NRR. "And Dan already unscrambled the letters."

Hamilton looked at the parchment suspiciously.

"Here's the thing," said Amy. "We can't visit all these places alone, and neither can you. What if we were to split them up? You go one way, we'll go the other, and we'll share what we find?"

Hamilton Holt's gelled slick of blond hair seemed to quiver as the gears in his brain started turning. He propped himself up on his elbow, and the look he gave Amy was almost imploring.

"And you can trust us," said Amy. "We're giving *you* the next place we're supposed to go. See that right there?" asked Amy, holding the parchment closer to Hamilton's face. "That's where we'll pick up the trail. In Omsk, Siberia."

Right beside the words Dan had added: "Next, at the crossroads of Y and Z." It made absolutely no sense whatsoever, but it sounded good, and Hamilton fell for it without hesitation. Dan figured he could give Hamilton the real instructions later, after he'd had more time to examine the treasure in his pocket.

"Here's what we're going to do," said Amy.

Amy told Hamilton to visit both Siberian outposts while she and Dan focused on the closer places. That left Moscow, Yekaterinburg, and St. Petersburg for Dan and Amy. They exchanged cell phone numbers and e-mail addresses.

"We'll swap information as we go and beat the pants off everyone else!" Dan hooted.

"That's if we don't kill ourselves getting down from here first," said Amy.

CHAPTER 5

Ian Kabra had been in the back of a limousine hundreds of times but never when covered in meat pies.

"The Holts are barbarians," he said disgustedly. He was sitting in the backseat, wiping beef stains off his five-thousand-dollar Armani suit.

"Here comes Hamilton!" said Natalie. She had fared better in the parking lot fight, retreating into the car at the first sign of flying food. She was never one to risk her Gucci.

"Driver, follow that piece of junk," said Ian. He pointed to the beat-up white van that Hamilton Holt had just dove into. The van rumbled to life and tore out of the lot.

Ian dialed his cell phone. The mere mention of the competition heading into Russia at such a sensitive juncture had sent his father into a panic. Now was not the time to take chances.

"What do you want?" The voice on the other end of the line belonged to Irina Spasky, the only Russian citizen on any of the teams. She, like Ian, was part of the Lucian branch. One rung *under* Ian and Natalie's parents, a fact that had long infuriated her.

"I don't know how you managed to let everyone into your country," said Ian. "But it's making my father nervous. And when he's nervous, *I'm* nervous. My father will have both our heads if we let another team capture one of our clues."

"They will not get anything!" snapped Irina. "It will be for them a wild geese chase."

Ian smirked. He could picture her eye twitching, as it always did when she was angry.

"I don't like all this activity so close to some very important secrets. It's your country. Deal with it."

"I suggest you hold your tongue. The line is not secure," said Irina.

"You follow Dan and Amy Cahill. I think they're on to something," Ian ordered. "We'll stay with the Holts."

"Agreed. You babysit the idiots. I will get the real work done."

Irina clicked off her cell phone and brooded in the backseat of a dingy Volkswagen van, the very one Dan and Amy had ridden from the airport. The bearded Russian was on the Lucian payroll, like hundreds of other informants spread across the homeland.

Who's helping Dan and Amy Cahill? she wondered. Could there be a double agent within the ranks of the Lucians? The idea had crossed her mind before, but with the death of Grace Cahill, her suspicions had grown. There were secrets in Russia—secrets that had to be protected at all cost. Dan and Amy had stumbled into a hornet's nest.

"They're on the move," said the bearded Russian in the front seat.

"Follow them," ordered Irina.

The driver merged into traffic and tracked a blinking dot on his screen.

"He's pretty good on that bike," said the driver, laughing despite the ultraserious agent sitting in the backseat of his van.

"I do not pay you for small talk," Irina fired back.

The bearded driver clammed up, and not another word was spoken during the drive through Volgograd. Irina felt the twitch in her eye return, soft at first but growing more violent. Twenty minutes passed before the driver spoke again.

"They've stopped. We're near the train station."

"Let me out," said Irina. A wad of bills rolled past the driver and landed at his feet.

"I may need you again," said Irina as she opened the door. "Keep your phone on and don't leave the city."

The driver nodded. He leaned down and picked the roll of bills off the floor. When he turned around again, Irina Spasky was gone.

"Are you positive we're going to the right place?" asked Amy.

"Yup," said Dan. Amy sighed, still not convinced they should have boarded the high-speed train. But Dan had been adamant about keeping the lead he'd found hidden until they were safely out of town. He was learning to be careful about who might be watching.

"Let's have a look at it," said Amy. "You've been holding out on me long enough."

Dan pulled the object he'd found in The Motherland Calls out of his front pocket. He glanced both ways down the center aisle of the train, then held it out to Amy.

"You can do the honors," said Dan. "I'm too tired to open it up."

Instead, he fished around in the backpack for some chips and pulled out Amy's Russian guidebook.

"This thing is crushing my snacks."

He set the book between them, cracked open a bag of pulverized Doritos, and disgusted his sister by tipping his head back and pouring the broken chips into his mouth.

Amy rolled her eyes and got back to the cylinder. It was wrapped in a tremendous amount of twine, so it was awhile before she finally parted the paper and held the secret object in her hand. It was a tiny statue intricately carved out of a hard orange substance, showing a bearded monk with wild eyes, standing with his arms folded in front of him.

Amy brightened. "I think I know who this is!"

"It's that dude who got us the motorcycle!" said Dan, peering over. He frowned. "Or maybe it's his brother."

Amy wasn't sure what to do with the precious carving. She was itching to refer to a certain page in the guidebook, but if she gave the carved monk to Dan, she worried he might drop it.

"Hold this," she said, succumbing to her desire for information. "And be careful. It's fragile."

"Got it covered," said Dan, snatching the carving from her and holding it up to the light.

"It's almost see-through," he said as Amy riffled through the book. "And there's something hidden inside."

"What?" asked Amy, reaching out for the carving.

"Whoa, there! Take it easy. This thing is *fragile*, remember?"

"What's in there? What do you see?"

"It's one of those pop-top games. I'm good at these. There's a little shoe, then two letters, a V and an A, then a heart."

"Shoevaheart," said Dan. "Is that something you've heard of?"

Amy shook her head no, but something about the word tugged at her. She thought for a minute, but nothing crystallized, so she showed Dan the picture she'd been looking for in the guidebook.

"It's Rasputin," said Amy. "I'm sure of it."

Dan looked at the photo, a grainy black-and-white of a man with furious eyes.

"Boy, these monk people sure get angry," he said. Amy knew he was thinking back to the mob of monks who had chased them in Austria. "Why so sure it's this guy?"

"Rasputin wasn't any ordinary monk. He was said to be almost impossible to kill. Doesn't that sound like something a Cahill would be? Un-killable?"

Dan's eyes widened.

"Rasputin worked his way into the inner circle of the most powerful Russian families ever: the Romanovs. They were royalty, like Princess Diana in England."

"Keep it coming, but no more princesses. You're starting to bore me."

"Rasputin was a real charmer. He convinced the royal family he had supernatural healing powers, and the evidence seems to suggest that he actually did."

"You're kidding," said Dan, looking almost as excited as when he realized his teacher was wearing a toupee.

"He was especially close to the heir to the throne, Alexei, and his sister Anastasia. She was amazing, trust me, but Alexei was constantly sick. He had hemophilia."

Dan pulled back. "Isn't that, like, something on your butt?"

"Gross! Not hemorrhoids, Dan! Hemophilia is a blood disorder. If Alexei got even the smallest cut, it wouldn't stop bleeding. So imagine like, I don't know . . . like if you fell off your skateboard and skinned your knee and it just bled and bled and bled until *all* your blood spilled out."

"Cool!" said Dan.

"*Not* cool! If it hadn't been for Rasputin, Alexei would have bled to death before he was ten. But *that's* not the most interesting part. There were a lot of nobles who didn't like the power Rasputin had over the royals, so they plotted to kill him."

"Okay, now this is getting good."

"Wait until you hear this," said Amy. She scanned the next part of the guidebook and put things into her own words. "On December 16, 1916, Prince Felix Yusupov invited Rasputin to a dinner party. First he fed Rasputin poisoned wine and cake, but that didn't seem to bother Rasputin at all. Rasputin figured out they were trying to kill him, so he ran for the door. Then Prince Felix shot Rasputin in the back."

"End of Rasputin. Too bad—I was starting to like the guy."

"Wrong! Rasputin kept on going, right up the stairs and out of the house. The prince's men shot him a few more times in the front yard, but Rasputin wouldn't die. They tied his hands and feet, stuffed him in a bag, and dropped him into an ice hole in a frozen river. And that finally did it. Rasputin suffocated under the ice." Amy's eyes gleamed and she lowered her voice. "But they say his fingernails were all worn off when they found him, like he tried to claw his way out for a half hour or more before finally giving up."

"That's the best story you've told me in your whole life," said Dan. "I don't even care if it's true or not."

"Dan, I think it *is* true. We of all people should believe it, even if history buffs don't buy it. Rasputin was a Cahill! Maybe we're even from the same branch of the family!"

"Like we could be superheroes!?!" Dan's eyes bugged out.

"Calm down," said Amy. "We still have to figure out where we're supposed to go in St. Petersburg once we get there."

Dan and Amy stopped talking, both lost in thought. And soon they were fighting sleep. The train had a maddening way of making a tired person even sleepier, the way it rocked and swayed, the clicking noise of the metal wheels on the track. Dan offered one last idea before conking out.

"Maybe we should go where they tried to kill Rasputin."

Amy batted that idea away. The carvings inside the figurine didn't match up with anything close to the Yusupov Palace. She stifled a yawn and kept digging, searching her book for anything related to a shoe or a heart. Her fingers floated up to her neck, and she absently rubbed the pendant on Grace's jade necklace.

Grace, what would you have done if you were me? she thought. Amy's eyes pooled with tears as Dan slept and the worries she tried to keep from him flooded in. She looked out across a glowing sunset.

I can't do this alone, she thought, flipping the Rasputin page in the Russian guidebook back and forth. One tear dropped, hitting the paper, and she wiped it away with a finger. Her eyes alighted on a word, and her mind turned it over, not wanting to let it go. And then out of nowhere she understood. It felt like a gift.

"I've got it! I've got it!" said Amy. Dan jerked awake and jumped to his feet in a ninja pose as Amy wiped the last of her tears away.

"There!" she said, pointing to a picture of the Yusupov Palace. "You were right, Dan!"

"Does this mean I get to go back to sleep?"

"Before the Yusupovs took over the palace, it was owned by someone else. Care to know who it was?"

"Enlighten me," said Dan, awake but with his eyes closed to the world.

"It was the mansion of Count Pyotr Shuvalov. Count Shoe-VA-Love. Don't you get it? A shoe, the letters VA, and the heart—Shuvalov."

"That sounds right," said Dan. Two seconds later, he bolted upright and turned to his sister with a big grin.

"Hey! You know what this means? You and I are on our way to the scene of a murder!"

Six rows back, Irina Spasky put down the newspaper she was hiding behind and frowned. She had walked past Dan and Amy's seat, shrouded in dark sunglasses and a low-brimmed hat, and planted a wireless mic. Every word, every stupid, dangerous idea Amy and Dan had discussed came through loud and clear.

The young Kabras are maniacs and the young Cahills are suicidal, she thought. *And now I must track them across Russia and protect old secrets instead of hunting down new clues.* She clicked her tongue in disgust and reflected on how much she disliked children. But her chest tightened in automatic protest. There was a child, a long, long time ago, she had liked very much.

CHAPTER 6

Sleeping on the train gave Dan and Amy an electric energy when they hit the pavement in St. Petersburg. Why go to a hotel when there were palaces to be broken into?

"We need to go that way," said Amy, the crisp evening air filling her with new excitement as she made her way down the bustling platform. They had arrived at Moskovsky Station, less than two miles from the palace, and decided to walk rather than risk another cab ride.

"There's a whole cluster of palaces along the banks of the Moika River. Yusupov is one of them."

"You should be a tour guide," said Dan. "Lead the way."

Soon they were outside following Nevsky Prospekt, an eight-lane avenue. Seventeenth-century pastel buildings and newly constructed stores stood side by side, competing for space in thriving twenty-first-century Russia.

"Dan," said Amy, jerking her brother's hand. "I think someone is tailing us."

Dan glanced over his shoulder.

"The man in black," he whispered.

It was unquestionably him. The dark coat and hat, the gliding way he moved, the craggy face full of shadows. He was unmistakable.

Amy and Dan broke into a run, darting between pedestrians on the busy sidewalk. Their movements seemed to set the world in motion. A truck barreled across two lanes, heading directly for them. Dan sped up, but Amy froze in her tracks. The truck swerved near the curb and an envelope came hurtling out the passenger window, landing in the gutter at Amy's feet.

"Watch where you're going, you big jerk!" yelled Dan. A lot of people turned to stare at him as the truck sped back into traffic and disappeared around a corner.

"He's gone," said Amy, her voice trembling in the night air. Had the man in black *made* the truck move? Either way, just as mysteriously as he had appeared, the man in black had vanished.

"I think we should keep going," said Dan. "That dude could be anywhere."

Amy nodded and they hurried down Nevsky Prospekt. Dan ripped open the envelope as they went.

"What's it say?" asked Amy.

As Dan read the letter aloud, Amy could almost feel the night getting blacker around them.

"'Time is running out. You need to move faster. You are being followed, and I don't mean the Madrigal.

When your pursuers show themselves, give them this map to throw them off track and be on your way. You must enter the palace at night and find Rasputin. Follow the orange snake. NRR.'"

"The man in black is a *Madrigal*! Do you realize what this means? We're dead. Dead, dead, dead!" Dan yelped.

"At least we got another note from NRR," said Amy. "We're hot on the trail of *something* . . . I just wish we knew what it was."

She put her hand on Dan's shoulder as if to steady both of them.

"I think we should keep going, don't you? It's not like we have a lot of choices here. And besides, the man in black is gone," Amy said.

"Okay, let's assume he's actually hit the road, which I doubt. So what? Apparently, there's someone else tailing us, not just him. It could be anyone, but it's probably someone who wants to *drop a piano on our heads*!"

"Chances are it's another team, that's all I'm saying. And besides, NRR gave us something to keep them busy."

"Maybe he wants to get us away from everyone else so we're an easier target," Dan argued. "Did you think of that? What if the picture of Mom and Dad is just a trick to get us totally off on our own?"

Amy paused. "Dan, I hate to tell you this, but we've been on our own for awhile now."

The truth of that silenced them both.

Amy took the letter from Dan. Across the bottom there was an elaborate map of St. Petersburg with a dotted line winding through it. It ended across two canals in an entirely different part of the city. Amy tore the map free from the rest of the letter.

"See? It looks like a trail leading somewhere important, but it's a wild goose chase. All we have to do is give it to whoever is tailing us when they show themselves, then they leave us alone for awhile. Maybe NRR is trying to isolate us, but the photo . . . I want to know what it means."

Amy could see Dan had run out of steam. He took a half-empty box of Skittles out of his back pocket and dumped about twenty of them in his mouth, chomping morosely.

"If we can just get inside the palace, I know what NRR means about Rasputin. There's a reenactment exhibit inside. It's all about when they tried to kill him, the stuff I was telling you," Amy coaxed.

"Suppose I gotta see that," said Dan, getting reluctantly excited again at the thought of an unkillable monk.

Amy smiled. "Okay! Now all we have to do is find a snake to follow."

It was nearly eleven o'clock by the time Dan and Amy approached Yusupov Palace. Things were starting to wind down along the quiet banks of the Moika, a river that ran along the front of the three-story palace of yellow and white. A few pedestrians strolled here and there along the embankment rail, and the occasional headlights came toward them, but other than that, the area was deserted.

The Yusupov Palace stretched along the river with thirty darkened windows on each level staring out onto the Moika. There was a giant arched entryway at the very center of the building, and three tall white columns on each side of the door.

"Somehow I don't think the door is going to be open," said Dan. "Should we try a window?"

Amy walked along the front of the palace, looking for anything that might resemble a snake.

"Amy," called Dan. He'd crossed the street to get a better look at the narrow river. It was only about sixty feet to the other side, where windowed buildings and houses lined a street similar to the one he stood on.

Amy arrived next to Dan and stared out into the black water.

"Do you see it?" asked Dan.

"See what?"

Dan pointed into the center of the waterway, where a glowing orange snake danced on the shimmering water. It was small, no more than a foot across. Dan followed a laser beam of light up and over the edge on the other side of the river. There, in one of the windows, he found what he was looking for: the shadow of someone in a room high above the water, pointing a laser out the window.

"It's moving," said Amy. And sure enough, when Dan looked back down, the orange snake was slithering across the water toward them.

"This is creepy," said Amy. "But cool. It's the kind of hint no one else can get. When it's gone, it's gone. If we can just follow it and get inside, no one else will know what to look for."

The orange snake had reached the embankment wall, and Dan and Amy had to lean over the rail to see it rising out of the water along the concrete slabs. As it came closer, they could tell it was no ordinary laser beam. It was moving a thousand times a second, creating a 2-D hologram of a snake as it slid along the stones.

"NRR has some cool toys," said Dan as the snake cleared the rail and arrived on the palace wall behind them.

"It's jumped the street!" said Amy. "We're going to lose it!"

The snake was moving faster now. It flew past the main door, along a row of windows, then crawled up the wall to the second story. When it hit the third window from the end, it slithered back and forth along the sill.

Amy glanced back in the direction of the window across the river. It made her nervous to think that someone was probably watching them through binoculars.

"Come on," Amy whispered, tearing her attention back to the palace. "I bet that window's our way inside."

Dan and Amy stood below the window, which was a good ten feet over their heads. The palace wall was as flat as a pancake.

"Even Spider-Man couldn't climb this thing," said Dan.

"Oh, yes he could," said Amy.

The orange snake had moved up another level, where a third row of windows hung low over a decorative façade. When the snake stopped, they heard a pop from the other side of the river. A split second later, something hit the façade and a spark flew.

"That thing is attached to a gun!" said Amy.

"Not a gun," Dan corrected her. "A gun would have been way louder. Look!"

A coil of rope was falling from where the snake had been. It rolled all the way down the side of the wall and dangled straight over the window they were to enter.

"Sweet!" said Dan.

"Dan, wait!" said Amy. She could hear a couple talking as they passed by, and a set of headlights was coming toward them.

"Just act casual," said Amy. "Pretend it's not there."

Dan and Amy started walking away from the rope until they passed the couple, nodding hello as they went. The car moved on as well.

"Um, Amy," said Dan.

"Yeah?"

"I think NRR wants us to get up that rope right now."

Dan was staring down at his own heart, where the orange snake had come to rest.

"The coast must be clear. He can see a lot better than we can from up there. Come on!"

Amy went first, holding the rope as she walked up the wall to the wide windowsill.

"Hurry, Dan!"

Amy pushed on the window, and it opened like a door on hinges. She darted through, leaning her head out to watch for cars as Dan pulled himself up.

"Headlights!" she said, grabbing Dan by his hoodie and yanking him inside. Dan lost his balance and toppled inside onto the marble floor, bashing his knee and howling in pain.

"Shhhhh!" said Amy, closing the window behind them. "There might be a security guard in the palace."

"I can't help it if you tried to break my neck getting in here!"

Dan stood up and tried to put pressure on his knee. "I'm going to have a monster bruise, but everything's still working. Where to now?"

"The main floor in the east wing," said Amy. "This way."

Amy had already scanned the guidebook and figured out the general location of the Rasputin exhibit. They passed through darkened rooms filled with expensive art and furniture.

"Looks like these royals liked nice stuff," said Dan.

"The Yusupovs were known for their good taste. They spent millions on redecorating and rebuilding projects."

As they made their way down a wide flight of purple-velvet-carpeted stairs, Amy heard a thump behind them.

"Did you hear that?" she asked.

"I think someone followed us in here. Hurry!"

Amy and Dan bolted down the stairs and turned a hard right. They passed under a tall archway and hung a left, ending up in front of a roped-off hallway.

"This is it," said Amy. She ducked under the rope and Dan followed. Another turn to the left and they arrived in an open, dimly lit room.

It was as if they'd stepped back in time to witness a murder. Everything from the night of Rasputin's death was meticulously re-created. There were sculptures and pictures, and best of all, two rooms with life-size wax figures.

"There he is," said Amy. In a room behind a yellow rope, Rasputin was sitting down at a table, eating the poisoned cakes that had been set before him.

"Come on, Dan. The trail leads to Rasputin. I'll check his pockets."

"I'll check under the table."

Amy braced herself and then reached into the thick black robes, her face just inches from Rasputin's wax head with its bushy beard and fixed, staring eyes.

A deep Russian voice behind her said, "You have made a grave error in coming here."

Dan tried to stand up from under the table and banged his head, sending saucers and cups clinking in the quiet room.

"Come away from there, both of you."

Dan recognized the voice immediately.

"Irina! What are you doing here?"

"Children do not outsmart me in my own country."

Dan looked at Amy and tried, without much luck, to read her frightened face. *Did you get anything?*

"Come, show me what you have found," said Irina. "I do not plan to hurt you."

Even in the shadowy light, Dan could see Irina was in her usual cheerless mood. He didn't trust her for one second.

"I think we'll stay right here if you don't mind," said Amy.

"Suit yourself. But you do not leave without answering a few questions. And you will give me what you have found."

Dan didn't have the map NRR had given them, and he wondered when Amy was going to spring it on Irina. *What's she waiting for?*

"Who is helping you?" asked Irina. She deliberately toyed with her fingernails, and Dan flinched at the reminder of the poison they contained.

"No one's helping us. We're just smarter than you are," said Dan, his eyes on his frozen sister.

"You think I didn't see the snake? You think I didn't hear everything you said on the train from Volgograd? You're not so smart, little man."

Dan started. *She's tailed us since Volgograd?!*

"You believe someone is trying to help you? *Ridiculous!*" continued Irina. "It's a trap! If you persist with this game, it will only lead to disaster. This person you are following? They will kill you once you've done their bidding."

Like you tried to kill us in Paris? thought Dan. He spotted a butter knife on the table and wondered if it would do any good to grab for it. If only he had real ninja moves.

"I ask you once more. Who is helping you?"

"Here," said Amy, finally emerging from her trance. She held out the map. "This is what we just found. You can have it. I haven't even looked at it yet. But can we at least *share* the information?"

Irina snatched the paper from Amy's hand and held it open in the soft light of the room. She let out a furious hiss.

"It is worse than I thought," she warned, raising her arctic eyes to the children. "You two are in grave danger. You *must* believe me. Tell me! Who is helping you?!"

For a second, Dan was almost taken in. He couldn't possibly trust her, and yet . . . something in her face registered a different kind of distress.

The moment passed in a flash, and Irina reverted to her typical grim resolve. She took a step toward Dan and Amy and curved one hand, her fingernail injectors gleaming menace.

"He didn't give us a name," said Dan. "We're following a lead, that's all. But if you don't share that piece of paper with us it's over. We'll lose the trail. Just tell us what it says and we'll go!"

Irina seemed *almost* satisfied. "If this person contacts you again, don't listen to him. He will kill you in the end. You must leave Russia and never come back. If you do not believe me, it is not my fault. But it is your death."

Irina backed off, shoving the map into her coat.

"Let's go, both of you. March!"

Dan and Amy hustled out of the exhibit with Irina close behind. She barked out directions until they reached the main entrance. Irina tapped out a code on her phone, held it up to an electronic alarm on the wall, and the huge wooden door clicked. She ushered Dan and Amy out into the cool night.

Once on the street, Irina hesitated, then seemed to make up her mind. "That map leads to secrets people would kill to protect," said Irina. She shut the door and started walking away. "Leave now, alive. Someday you'll thank me."

Dan and Amy watched her leave with open mouths, feeling like two small fish that have watched a great white shark swim by. Then they came to their senses and hustled along the canal in the opposite direction. When Dan was sure they'd lost Irina, he put a hand on Amy's arm.

"Did you find what NRR wanted us to find?"

He held his breath. If Amy hadn't discovered anything hidden on Rasputin, they were at a dead end.

"I got it," said Amy. "And that's not all. There was something about the exhibit that's got me very curious. I think we're one step closer to figuring out who NRR is."

Amy reached into her pocket and pulled out the next piece of the puzzle.

CHAPTER 7

Amy was fine with a little bit of luxury if the opportunity presented itself, but the Russians took decadence to a whole new level.

"How did I ever let you talk me into this?" she asked, staring at a grand piano in the middle of their hotel suite. They'd taken the risk of hailing a cab, after which Dan had held up his Visa gold card and said, "Take us to the best hotel in St. Pete's."

They'd arrived at the Grand Hotel Europe, one of the fanciest hotels in all of Russia. But as they entered the $2,000-a-night suite, Dan decided it wasn't up to snuff.

"What a rip-off!" said Dan. "Sixty-eight thousand rubles and there's no pinball machine?"

Dan raced from room to room, past all the expensive furniture and paintings.

"They don't even have a big-screen TV or a Coke machine!"

"It has two nice big beds *and* unlimited room service. Works for me," said Amy, rubbing a small item

between her fingers. It was the object she'd discovered in Rasputin's pocket at the palace: an oblong wooden token painted with a coat of arms and a set of words:

She'd understood the words right away, a reference to one of her favorite books. _Criminals be not punished_ here had to mean Dostoevsky's classic _Crime and Punishment_. Amy loved her books big and sprawling, and this thing was a doorstop.

It was Dan, with his keen eye and incredible memory, who had recognized the coat of arms. The Russian guidebook had a whole section on heraldry. He'd correctly identified this one as belonging to Omsk, the very place the Holts were headed. Too bad they were being tailed by the Kabras.

Amy pulled out Nellie's phone and charger and searched for an outlet. They'd been too busy to contact Nellie, and the growing guilt had been knotting Amy's stomach for hours.

"I can't believe we let her worry about us for the entire day and night. For all she knows, we're still out looking for doughnuts in Cairo."

When she glanced over, she saw that Dan was on the hotel phone dialing room service. He had a giant

English-Russian menu spread across his lap. Amy shook her head as she plugged in the phone and watched the little screen do its start-up dance.

"You don't have PB and J on the menu, either? Rich people food is no fun!" said Dan. He'd also asked for orange soda, chocolate chip cookies, and onion rings.

"I'm calling Nellie," Amy interrupted. "Do you want to listen in?"

"Hang on," said Dan. He hung up, grabbed his laptop and the power cord, and joined Amy on the floor. The two of them sat next to each other, the wall outlet between them.

"All this beautiful furniture and we're sitting on the floor. What's wrong with us?" asked Amy.

"I guess we're not too good at living the high life. Good thing. Wouldn't want to end up like the Cobras."

Amy couldn't help thinking Dan had fallen under the spell of a Visa gold card pretty quickly.

"Dan, look at this. She's got messages."

The voice mail light blinked green on Nellie's phone. Amy pressed the RETRIEVE button and activated the tiny speakerphone.

"You have seven new messages," a female voice offered.

Amy pressed the 7 key and the first message came through, although it was a bad connection and they couldn't catch the entire thing.

"If you guys . . . CALL ME! It's taking a long . . . get those doughnuts. The hotel number is . . ." The message crackled so badly at the end they couldn't decipher the rest.

Five more messages were of equally lousy quality, all from Nellie, her voice becoming more concerned with each effort to reach them.

"She's going to kill us," said Dan.

"You got that right," Amy agreed.

She clicked to retrieve the last message. It wasn't from Nellie.

"Call in for a status report," said a man's whispery voice. "We haven't heard from you."

Dan and Amy stared at each other.

"Do you know who that was?" asked Amy. "It's not a voice I've ever heard, have you?"

"No," Dan said, and shook his head hard, as if trying to knock a bad thought out of it. They stared at each other for a second, and then Amy deliberately changed the subject.

"I hope Nellie is okay. I'm worried about her."

"I wonder how Saladin is doing," said Dan, a glint of concern rising in his voice.

"Let's e-mail her instead of calling," said Amy. "Just let her know we're okay. That way we don't have to worry about her freaking out on us. I'm not sure I could handle that right now."

"And we'll tell her to take good care of Saladin," said Dan.

They jumped online and found a string of e-mails from Nellie that sounded a lot like the phone messages she'd left. She was careful to let them know that Saladin was doing just fine, dining on fresh fish from a Cairo marketplace and taking long naps in the hotel room.

"You see there?" said Amy. "Saladin is doing great."

Amy took the laptop and banged out a short message.

```
Dear Nellie, We stumbled onto a trail we
couldn't turn back from. Before we knew it,
we were on our way out of Cairo and into
Russia. It all happened really fast. We know
you probably can't come get us, but don't
worry — we're okay. No problems so far. Please
take good care of Saladin. We promise to
check back in tomorrow morning. Please don't
worry — we're fine! Amy and Dan.
```

"How's that?" asked Amy.

"I think it'll do the trick. Send it."

Amy clicked the SEND button. At least Nellie would know they weren't dead.

"We should send something to Hamilton, too, don't you think?" asked Dan.

Amy had almost forgotten. Of course! The trail led into Siberia next, right where Hamilton Holt would arrive by early morning on the Trans-Siberian Railway. She started typing out a message as Dan retrieved Hamilton's e-mail address from their backpack.

Hamilton — Your turn. We've found the next item and it leads right to where you're going. When you get to Omsk, look for a statue of Dostoevsky. He's a famous Russian writer, so if you ask around you shouldn't have any trouble locating him. Here's the important thing: You have to figure out what Dostoevsky is looking at. Follow his eyes. Whatever he's staring at is the next thing on our hunt. Our guess is it will lead back toward us. Let's stay ahead of the competition! Call our cell when you figure this out. Amy and Dan.

"It's ringing," said Dan. Nellie's phone was vibrating softly on the carpeted floor. Dan looked at the screen.

"It must be Nellie. She must have been sitting by a computer just waiting for us to contact her. That's good, right?"

But Amy wasn't so sure. She was exhausted, and the man's whispering voice from Nellie's phone seemed to reach for her. *Call in for a status report. We haven't heard from you.*

"Let it ring," she said. "Let's get some sleep."

When Dan woke up, Amy was gone. For a split second he freaked out, running back and forth between rooms until he saw the note stuck to the post of his bed.

My mom made us put these stupid things on
for a family picture. She said it would make
the perfect Christmas card. Whatever. Not
exactly cold in Siberia this time of year, so
we ditched the jackets. Dad's off looking for
meat pies, Mom and the twins are looking for
a bathroom. I just got service on my laptop
again—spotty out here in the tundra, har-har,
but I got your message. I'm at an Internet
café. Had no trouble getting directions to
this Dostrovinsky statue. Dude's got a weird
name, but that helped, because someone here
at the café already told me where to find
it. Lucky me, it's right around the corner.
I'll check out where the guy is looking and
get right back to you. Cell phone service is
choppy, but I might get a bar or two once
I'm out in the open air again. On the hunt
—Hammer.

"Hammer?" said Dan. "He's kidding, right?"

"It must be a family nickname."

Dan stuffed a wad of pancake in his mouth and
held his fork high in the air.

"Beware fellow contestants—the Hammer is on the
case!"

They were both giggling when they heard Nellie's
phone vibrating again.

"I think we better answer it this time," said Dan, all the wind gone out of his sails.

Amy walked to the phone and picked it up. Unknown caller ID. She decided it was time to do some talking.

"Hello?" said Amy, picking up the phone.

"Amy? Is that you, Amy?" Nellie's excited voice flooded across the line. She sounded overjoyed.

"It's me, we're okay!" said Amy.

"Yes, yes, YES! Is Dan there? IS HE SAFE?"

"Dan's okay, as long as he doesn't explode from eating too many pancakes."

"I was worried SICK about you two," said Nellie. "And Saladin won't stop crying. He misses you guys. Russia? ARE YOU KIDDING ME?! How COULD you let this happen?"

"How's Saladin?" asked Dan.

Amy waved him off as Nellie continued to rant.

"I don't know what's gotten into you two! STAY PUT until I get there. I've already grabbed a flight to Moscow. Where are you exactly?"

Amy tried to do the math in her head . . . Moscow to St. Petersburg . . . probably an overnight train. It was a long time to wait.

"We're in St. Petersburg, but we have to keep moving, Nellie," said Amy. "This hunt we're on is time sensitive. I don't think we can sit here and do nothing all day."

Another call was trying to break in. It was Hamilton Holt.

"Listen, Nellie, I've got to go. Come to Moscow and we'll call you as soon as we can. Hold tight."

"NO WAY! Stay where you a—"

Amy clicked the phone and switched calls. Hamilton started yelling into the phone so loudly Dan could hear it from across the room.

"I see it! I see what that author dude is staring at!"

"Good job, Hamilton! What is it? What's he looking at?"

Dan sidled up next to Amy so he could listen in.

"Dad! I got this!"

It sounded like Eisenhower Holt was trying to grab the phone. Amy heard Mary-Todd yell something in the background.

"Hey! Let go of that parka!"

Reagan and Madison were howling somewhere close by.

"He's looking at the ground!" Hamilton yelled. "It's all bricks, and one of them says something on it. It says—"

"Hamilton? What's it say?"

"It says 'Alexei's Playroom,' and there's a little symbol here, looks like a six-sided gem."

"You didn't tell the Kabras, did you?"

"Those losers? No way," said Hamilton.

"Great job, Hamilton! You did it! Um . . . await further instructions."

"You got it . . . Dad! Yo, Dad! This is getting WAY out of hand. Hammer Holt, signing off!"

The phone went dead and Amy raced across the room for the Russian guidebook.

"This confirms my suspicions," said Amy, riffling through pages, searching, searching, searching. . . .

She lifted gleaming eyes to Dan. "Get the backpack. We've got a royal village to visit!"

CHAPTER 8

Amy Cahill had been ripped off, bugged, double-crossed, and taken advantage of one too many times. She was *through* with taking taxicabs.

"I have a better idea," said Dan. He put his beatnik goatee and mustache on and walked right up to the hotel bank, flashing a smile along with his passport and Visa gold card.

"I need a cash advance. Can you dig it?"

Amy had to stifle a laugh. Did Dan actually think he was going to get real money with a line like that?

"We have fee of one thousand rubles on American cards," said the teller. One thousand rubles was about thirty bucks, which sounded like a lot of money to Amy. Then again, it was NRR's money, not hers, and they'd just racked up more than $2,000 on their bill.

"That'll be fine," Dan replied. "And, ah, tip yourself another thousand while you're at it. I'll take a hundred thousand for myself if the card will hold it. Been spending like a sailor on leave. I must be getting close to the limit on that thing."

Dan laughed as if he didn't really care, but Amy knew better. They'd had to count every penny back home.

"Ahhh, is good for you," said the man, suddenly Dan's best friend. "In American dollars you have balance of six thousand. The card has forty-four thousand unused. But you know the limits of your own credit, of course."

"FORTY-FOUR THOUSAND!" Dan choked back a cough of surprise, then asked for an additional 100,000 rubles, just in case. He leaned in close to Amy and whispered, "If rubles are anything like marbles, my backpack is going to be really heavy."

The teller counted out the bills. The stack, amounting to about 7,500 American dollars, was so tall it teetered back and forth as he reached the final 1,000. Dan's eyes got huge and he tipped the teller another 1,000.

"Very kind, sir, very generous. Thank you! I wish you and your young friend a good day."

Amy's jaw dropped as she realized that in disguise, Dan probably looked a lot older than she did.

"He's *not* older than me!" she said without thinking.

Dan smirked and leaned in close to the teller.

"You know how sensitive little sisters can be. She's impossible."

"Keep it up, buddy," Amy said under her breath, "and I'll tear that fake mustache right off your dumb face."

As soon as they got out of the lobby and into the street, Amy hammered Dan with questions. "What in the world do you want with all that money?"

"I got a plan," said Dan.

"A *plan*? You're eating *way* too much candy and it's turning your head fizzy." Carrying around gobs of money made her nervous.

"There, that looks like the perfect fit for our needs," said Dan.

Dan was watching a middle-aged man get out of a car. It was the smallest car Amy had ever seen, more like a go-cart, really. And it was blue, which made Amy nervous. Blue was Dan's favorite color.

"Time to start my car collection!" said Dan. "Come on. This is going to be awesome."

"You're so much dumber than I thought," Amy groaned. "And that's saying something. Do you remember that *neither one of us knows how to drive*?"

But Dan bolted across the street and hailed the man. The guy was bald as a potato, with stains on his tie and an attitude of being late for something important.

"How much for the car?" asked Dan. "I'm in a rush and I've got cash."

The man glanced at Dan, saw how small he was, and let out a sharp hoot of a laugh. "Stupid Americans! Go home!"

"See this backpack?" Dan said, trailing after him. "It's full of cash! I'm serious here!"

The man couldn't seem to help himself and turned back. "How much in rucksack? Tiny Tim not cheap," he said.

Tiny Tim?! thought Amy. "Wait a sec—"

"Enough," said Dan, talking over her. "I'll give you, um, let's see . . . how about twenty thousand rubles for it?"

Amy coughed up a weird yelping sound, as if there were a hair ball stuck in her throat. The idea of spending twenty thousand *anything* was outrageous.

"Thirty," said the man, fiddling with his tie and looking at Dan sideways.

Dan hauled bills out of the backpack.

"You know how to drive Russian car?" asked the man, beaming. "I show you!"

Dan beamed right back. "You got yourself a deal."

A few minutes later, the potato-headed man had taken his thirty thousand rubles, happy as a clam, and given Dan and Amy a five-minute tour of Tiny Tim. It wasn't much bigger than a refrigerator, and it only had two gears: slow and fast.

"Leave stick up until Tiny is twenty-five, then slam it down, like so." The man grabbed the stick shift and yanked it back about a foot. "No . . . how you say . . . clatch?"

"Clutch," corrected Amy, sounding more interested in Tiny Tim.

"Little sister is rude," said the man.

"You said it," offered Dan, running his fingers through the fake goatee. Amy thought she might explode.

The man pointed to the pedals on the floor in front of the driver's seat. "That is brake, that is gas. Easy!"

"Seems simple enough," said Dan. Amy still couldn't believe they'd just bought a go-cart masquerading as an automobile.

"I am late," said the man, patting his pocket to make sure the money was still there. "Be careful. Tiny is faster than he looks. He will make man out of you. *Da svidanya!*"

"Dude, I'm *so* driving this thing," said Dan. Amy gritted her teeth. She hated it when he called her dude. It made absolutely *no sense*.

Dan grinned. "We've got a boatload of money and our own car! This is incredible."

"Yeah," said Amy. "Incredibly *stupid*."

Dan looked wounded. "It's not stupid. Every time we use the card, NRR can track us. Now we're like outlaws—cash only and a cool ride of our own. Untraceable."

Amy had to concede the point, but there was no way she was letting her eleven-year-old brother drive her around Russia.

"Move over, Richie Rich. I've practically got a learner's permit already. I can do this."

Dan protested until his mustache fell off, but Amy wasn't budging. She settled into the driver's seat, her nerves starting to get the best of her.

Dan hopped back on the offensive. "You absolutely sure you can do this? I've got experience on the streets of Russia. Maybe you should let the exp—"

"Just stop talking and let me concentrate, will you?"

"Oh, yeah, you sound *really* ready to drive," said Dan, strapping a tattered old seat belt across his waist.

That did it. Amy had had enough. She turned the key and the tailpipe coughed out a plume of smoke. The engine rumbled and popped as if it wanted nothing more than to race through traffic.

"Okay," said Amy, taking a deep breath and setting her foot on the pedal. "Here goes thirty thousand rubles."

Tiny Tim lurched along the side of the road doing about three miles an hour until Amy caught the hang of it and sped up to ten. Pretty soon she was doing twenty.

"You like Tiny Tim, don't you?" said Dan. "Come on, let me drive it. Please?"

"Eat your heart out, *dude*," said Amy. "Just keep the directions coming and don't distract me."

Dan grumbled, but he found the dog-eared map of St. Pete in the guidebook. A smile bloomed on Amy's face. When the speedometer hit 25, she slammed the stick shift down and Tiny Tim lurched forward with a sharp buzzing sound.

"Wow! He's got some giddyup!" said Amy.

Tiny Tim swerved back and forth as Amy tried to find the brake pedal.

"Amy," said Dan. "You see the telephone pole, right? AMY!"

Amy jerked the steering wheel hard to the left, narrowly avoiding the sidewalk.

"C-c-calm down, Tiny Tim!" yelled Amy. She finally found the brake pedal, tapping it softly a few times and bringing the car under control.

"I think I'm getting the hang of it," she said.

Amy glanced at Dan. He looked as miserable as the time Aunt Beatrice confiscated his nunchucks. But he dutifully gave directions, asking questions as they went.

"Tell me again why we're going to this village of royals."

"*The royal village.* In Russia they call it Tsarskoye Selo, the Tsar's Village. It's where the Romanovs went on holiday."

"And why do we care about the Romanovs again?" asked Dan.

"They were the last royal family in Russia. This is the family Rasputin held so much sway over."

Amy had settled onto a long highway doing about forty. As they headed for the Tsar's Village, she told Dan all about the last Russian royal family.

How they'd been overthrown and banished to the village. One day they were the most powerful family in Russia, the next they were prisoners. Amy was especially interested in the young grand duchess Anastasia. Everything Amy had read about her was fantastic. Anastasia was raised as a normal child, not like a royal, and she was exceptionally charming. She was also brilliantly naughty, always playing pranks on her teachers and friends.

"She liked to play all sorts of tricks, and apparently she was a great climber of tall trees. Once she was up a tree it was hard to get her to come down."

"Sounds like my kind of kid," said Dan.

"But she came to an awful end. She was murdered, Dan. They all were. Her brother, Alexei, and her three sisters. And her parents. It was a firing squad, bullets flying everywhere, ricocheting off walls. But there's a bright spot, something I think is connected to all this. There are a lot of people who think Anastasia didn't die with the rest of her family."

"When did she die, then?"

"Who knows? But some say when they went to examine the grave site years later, her body wasn't there."

"Cool!" said Dan.

"You know what I think? I think Rasputin was a Cahill. I think he might have tried to save Alexei and Anastasia. Maybe he gave them whatever it was that made him so hard to kill. First Alexei, to cure him of his illness, then Anastasia, to save her from a firing squad. Maybe they *couldn't* kill her."

Dan was silent, his eyes huge, and Amy knew he was lost in superhero daydreams again.

Super Dan. That's all *I need.*

They kept driving in silence as St. Petersburg disappeared and the countryside started to take over. Rolling hills on either side marked their way, and with the windows rolled down, they smelled the fresh air.

"The village was one of the last places where Alexei and Anastasia played. Alexei's playroom was a favorite place in the palace. And I'll tell you something else. Right before they took her, at the very end, Anastasia and her sisters hid their most valuable jewels. They sewed them into their clothes so no one could find them."

"How'd you know about that?" Dan said, turning toward her with a skeptical look. "Don't tell me this guidebook has a section on hiding valuables."

"Wikipedia," said Amy. "I checked it out while you were sleeping. They hid a lot of jewels in the hems of their dresses and pants. Hamilton Holt said that at the Dostoevsky statue there was a jewel on the brick along with the words *Alexei's Playroom.* I think we should keep our eyes peeled for an article of clothing in this playroom. I bet that's where we'll find what we're looking for."

The royal village was coming into view and Amy tapped on the brakes, shifting Tiny Tim into low gear as it spluttered to a crawl.

"Let's leave Tiny as far away from the security guards as possible. I'd hate to see him get towed away."

They parked the car and walked along a lengthy row of gardens and opulent buildings. Grand white fountains trickled everywhere and the flowing lawns were perfectly trimmed.

"Pretty nice place to be banished," said Dan. "It's not exactly a prison cell."

"No kidding," said Amy. The royal village was even more spectacular than Amy had imagined. She'd seen pictures, but they hadn't come close to capturing the endless lawns and beautiful buildings.

"That one is Catherine Palace," said Amy, pointing to a building that went on for what seemed like a mile.

"The Russians like their buildings long," said Dan. Catherine Palace looked to Dan like an extended dollhouse. It was bright blue with white accents and gold trim, about fifty feet tall and ten times as long.

"And that's our destination," said Amy, pointing down the long row of gardens in the center of the royal village. "Alexander Palace. Come on, maybe we can get in and out fast."

Alexander Palace was completely different from Catherine Palace. Ancient white columns of stone stood before pale yellow walls that seemed to go on forever in a wide U-shape. Behind the circular driveway lay a sprawling green lawn leading to a shimmering pond.

"I hope you know where we're going," said Dan. "This place is gigantic. It could take hours to find one room."

"I've got it covered," said Amy. She had taken down notes on a piece of hotel stationery, which she pulled out of her pocket.

"According to a travel blog I read, Alexei's Playroom is on the second floor in the children's wing. We go past the Crimson Room, which will put us in the Marble Hall, then to a Portrait Hall . . ."

Amy kept reading off elaborate directions until they arrived at the arched front door and entered the palace. A uniformed tour guide nodded and smiled.

"Can you point us in the direction of Alexei's Playroom?" asked Dan.

"Certainly." The man turned and pointed to a wide set of stairs. "Up there, down hall, left. Is great room."

Amy put away her directions and scowled at Dan. "Show-off."

Within minutes, they were standing at the doorway of one of the most incredible playrooms Amy had ever seen.

"This kid had it good," said Dan. "I'd never leave unless I had to eat or use the bathroom."

Alexei's Playroom was a vast space filled with handmade toys of every imaginable kind. There was a miniature tepee at the center of the room with two child-size canoes standing by. An elaborate train set with tracks running every which way, a giant stuffed sheepdog, sailing ships, and crates of blocks. The ceiling was hung with airplanes and gliders, and toy houses lined one entire wall.

"I don't see any clothes, do you?" asked Amy. The exhibit was designed to allow viewers to walk through the middle of the playroom on a narrow red carpet and exit on the other side.

"Come on," said Dan. "Let's get a closer look."

"Your parents are nearby?"

Amy was on edge already and the voice startled her. When she turned, she saw that the tour guide from downstairs had followed them up.

"Children are not allowed without parents. Little hands are tempted."

Amy wished Dan had left the goatee on, but it was too late now.

Dan glanced at her, then started talking. "This whole vacation has been the pits. *Booooring*. Just our luck we finally find something really cool and we can't go inside."

Amy caught on quickly and jumped in. "Our mom and dad are still over at Catherine Palace, looking at paintings. Ugh."

The tour guide seemed to understand.

"My children love this room also."

"Can you take us in?" pleaded Dan.

The tour guide glanced back down the hall. It was early yet and the palace was relatively empty. No one else appeared to be coming.

"Hands in pockets, please! No touching!"

Amy and Dan reluctantly pocketed their hands, and the tour guide entered the room in front of them. He was showing them the ships when a rambunctious set of very young British children appeared in the doorway.

"Mummy! Look at the toys!" yelled one of them, and they were off on a tear, heading straight for the tepee.

"Stop! Stop! Stay on red carpet!" protested the tour guide. The parents tried to intervene, but the two children raced from one item to the next, just out of reach of the guide.

This is my chance, thought Amy, spying a closet door. Dan stood his ground, trying his best to obscure her escape from the chaos in the room. Before the guide could turn around, Amy had slipped into the closet and closed the door.

It was dark inside but for a sliver of light seeping through the bottom of the doorway. Amy felt around and discovered that the closet was full of hanging clothes. Could these really be items from such a long time ago? Her fingers searched through silky soft and lacy cloth for a jewel along the hems. She reached into a pocket and latched her fingers around something hard. It was small and round, solid and firm, but when she lifted it out and held it close, she felt a fizzy sting in her nose.

Mothball!

"Eeeww," she whispered, dropping the round white ball back in the pocket where she'd found it. Amy dug her fingers into all the pockets she could find: nothing but more mothballs and pieces of fuzz.

The sound of the tour guide's muffled voice returned.

"Where is sister?"

"She's gone up ahead. I think I'll do the same," said Dan.

Amy's eyes were beginning to adjust to the darkness as she kept at it, scrunching each article of clothing between her fingers. She couldn't be sure, but it seemed as if the tour guide was still just outside the door, making sure everything was properly in place.

What's this? She had reached into the back of the closet to feel along the hem of a child's dress. Amy got down on her hands and knees and crawled in deeper, keeping a tight grip on the small lump she'd discovered.

Just then, the handle on the closet door turned and the door opened. Amy stayed perfectly still at the back of the closet, hidden in the forest of coats and dresses. She could see the silhouette of the tour guide.

"Any chance you could let me have a closer look at the train? I'm big into railroads."

It was Dan, who'd come back into the room in the nick of time.

"Oh. Yes," said the tour guide. "But then I must find others. Bad children should be kept on leash!"

The closet door closed once more and Amy breathed a sigh of relief. She tore at the hem of the dress, feeling terrible for having to damage such a precious item. For all she knew, it had actually been worn by the grand duchess Anastasia herself. The mere thought of it made her hands shake.

"Got it!" she whispered, feeling the smooth stone between her fingers. She placed it in her pocket, returned to the door, and listened for voices. It sounded as if they'd gone.

"Dan?" she whispered, opening the closet door a tiny crack and peering into the room. The door burst open and Amy fell forward, landing hard on the floor and nearly crushing a toy playhouse filled with miniature figurines.

"I knew it!" said the tour guide.

Dan sprang into action, jumping on the stuffed sheepdog. "Ride 'em!" he called. Amy's eyes bugged out. Her brother was always ready to humiliate himself for a cause.

The tour guide marched toward Dan, his jaw clenched. Amy bolted for the exit, running as fast as she could. "C'mon, Dan!"

She didn't have to wait long.

"Run!" Dan howled. "He's right on my tail!"

Amy and Dan shot down the staircase with the tour guide close behind.

"Don't stop, Amy! Just keep going!" said Dan. Tour guides were converging from three directions now, but

Dan and Amy were just fast enough to reach the front door of the palace first. They dashed out into the bright light of the sunny Russian morning and kept right on going.

"Do not come back!" yelled the tour guide they'd tricked. He stood fuming between his two coworkers. "Children! They will kill me!"

Amy and Dan slowed to a walk and caught their breath. Before long, they were convulsed with laughter.

"I found some candy in there," said Amy. "Kept it for you."

She held out a round white mothball, but Dan wasn't taking the bait.

"You first!"

Amy wound up and threw the mothball toward the pond. She'd driven a car for the first time, touched the clothes of a princess, and found their next lead — it was a great morning by anyone's standards.

CHAPTER 9

Irina Spasky's thumb hovered over the SEND button on her phone. She couldn't seem to bring herself to make the call. She took a deep breath and put the phone back in the pocket of her thin black coat. *The Kabras can wait*, she thought, turning away from Alexander Palace. Irina began to walk, alone as usual, toward the pond at the other side of the palace grounds.

She had watched Dan and Amy enter the palace, seen them run out toward that wreck of a car they'd purchased. They had been *laughing*. That bothered her. They were happy, these two. They would get into their tiny automobile and continue on until, eventually, they would lead Irina to trouble of the worst kind. *A Lucian double agent. Perhaps a Madrigal.*

They'd found something in the palace, this much was obvious. They were in deeper trouble than they realized.

It doesn't have to end badly, she tried to convince herself. Another child flashed before her eyes, younger, blonder. *Why do I remember him best as a toddler?*

She remembered little of the last days, and almost nothing about the funeral. Almost everything had faded away but the weather. She would never forget the low, oppressive clouds and soft snow as they lowered the casket into the ground. Since then, there had been too many days and nights alone, too much time to think, and far too much compromised. *Lose a child, and you lose your soul.*

Irina took the phone in her hand again and this time she didn't hesitate to press the button.

"Finally," snapped Ian Kabra. "Have we got anything to worry about?"

"Yes," said Irina. She'd arrived at the pond and stood staring into the algae-covered water. "Someone helps them. Someone high up in the Lucian branch. It must be."

"What makes you think so?" Ian asked.

"They've just left Alexei's Playroom. They must know about the Lucian connection to the Romanovs."

"Make sure they don't find themselves in possession of sensitive material. You know what's at stake. One step closer and you'll have to remove them."

"I know."

Irina paused, but the temptation to goad was too strong.

"It won't be just me your father punishes," she warned softly, and clicked off her phone.

At least she wasn't being asked to do anything too drastic to the children yet. She took a device out of her pocket and turned it on. A small screen came to life.

"Where are you off to now, Dan and Amy Cahill?" she said.

Irina had already placed the coordinates from the parking lot into the device. A distant satellite beamed images onto her screen, zooming in closer and closer until the top of a blue car came into view.

"Not bad," Irina said, pleased with the clever device the Lucians had only recently put into use in the field. The car was blurry and lacking detail on the screen, but the tiny blue top was unmistakable.

This will be easier than I thought.

Irina got in her own car, keeping the blue on-screen as she took chase. Two minutes later, the small car turned right.

"Off the main road," she mumbled, seeing Dan and Amy turn off the highway. "You two are full of surprises."

A few minutes later, Irina had unexpectedly caught up, finding herself on a one-lane dirt road. She no longer needed the satellite viewer because she was quickly overtaking the small car. She hadn't intended to get so close to Amy and Dan, and she certainly didn't want them spotting her. But the road was narrow, with plowed-over fields on both sides, and she had a big car. What was worse, the blue car had stopped and was turning around.

This will be complicated, thought Irina as the little car zoomed closer. It was going way too fast, as if the driver was planning to slam right into her front grill. Irina threw her car into reverse and began backing down the dirt road.

"Stop, you maniacs!" she screamed. Her car fishtailed violently, caught the edge of a big rock, and spun out into the thick, tilled farmland.

The blue car buzzed up to Irina and screeched to a halt. Its driver was a gray-bearded man whose smile revealed a missing front tooth.

"Who gave you this car? Where did they go?" Irina screeched in Russian, rolling down her window.

The man nodded with some enthusiasm, which made Irina wonder if he had understood her questions. She peered into the empty backseat.

"Tell me, you idiot!" Irina screamed.

The name-calling seemed to upset the driver and his smile evaporated. "Americans," he began. "Gave me ten thousand rubles plus the car in exchange."

"Exchange for what?" yelled Irina.

"My truck," said the man.

"What color was the truck? Which way did they go? *Skazhi!*"

Irina should have known better than to hound an old Russian farmer. He was not amused by her angry tone, and he stared into the farmland as if he were made of iron.

Irina reached into her pocket and pulled out a small revolver. Her eye was twitching furiously, but when she turned back to the car it widened in shock. The old farmer had slammed his foot down on the gas pedal, shooting a plume of dust and mud through her open window.

Chunks of farm road flew into Irina's face. She threw her car into gear and hit the gas, but the soft tilled earth she'd backed into gave way and her rear wheels dug in.

She was stuck.

Irina coughed and spit, trying to clear all the mud from her mouth. The gunk in her eyes and mouth wasn't nearly as bad as the awful truth.

I've lost them.

"Do you think we've lost her for good?" asked Dan. It had been his idea to enlist the help of the farmer walking along the dirt road. Dan's backpack full of money was coming in handy in more ways than he could have imagined.

"I have no idea, but I don't think I can stay in here much longer. Tiny Tim's trunk is like a mailbox and your feet stink."

"I hate to break the news, but it's your feet that stink, not mine," said Dan.

Amy sniffed.

"Actually, I think it's the farmer. He needs a bath."

Tiny Tim slowed to a crawl and turned a hard right. A few seconds later it stopped and the trunk popped open.

"You pay now?" asked the farmer.

"We pay now," answered Dan, crawling out of the trunk and peering around him. Amy came out next and ran for the driver's seat before Dan could beat her to it. She caught his eye in the rearview mirror and stuck out her tongue.

When Dan got in the car after paying the farmer, he made his broccoli face.

"Next time, let's get help from someone who hasn't been walking around in cow manure all day," said Amy. They rolled down the windows and Amy hit the gas as the old man wandered into the open farmland, counting his rubles.

Amy was pushing Tiny Tim as fast as it would go, straight for the airport in St. Petersburg. She assumed they'd need to visit one of the two non-Siberian places left on their hunt: Moscow or Yekaterinburg.

As the little car strained along, Dan juddered in his seat, holding the honey-colored stone Amy had discovered in Alexei's closet. It was an oval, about two inches around and flat like a skipping rock.

"No way this thing was missed all those years," said Dan. "NRR had to put it there for us."

"I agree. I just wish what was inscribed made more sense. He's not making it easy on us."

"No kidding."

Dan looked carefully at each of the elements on the stone and tried to piece them together. It was just the kind of thing he should be able to figure out.

"A pile of bones, the number fifty-two, an arrow, and the letters M and S separated by a comma. Cryptic to say the least."

"Is the arrow pointing toward the M and the S or away from them?" asked Amy.

"Away from them," answered Dan. "And the bones, now that I get a better look at them, are cracked. These are broken bones."

Amy slammed on the brakes *way* too hard and Tiny Tim swerved along the shoulder of the road. Cars honked from behind and Dan came inches from smacking his head against the windshield.

Drivers passed by, screaming abuse and honking their horns. Amy tried to catch her breath; the near accident had really shaken her up.

"You almost sent me through the windshield!" Dan yelled.

Then his eyes lit up and he turned to his sister. "My turn to drive?"

Fifty yards up was a tree-lined side road that looked much more calm than the two-lane highway. Amy put

Tiny Tim into low gear, crawled to the turn, and drove another hundred yards before swinging a U-turn and parking on the side of the road. She'd finally calmed down enough to talk.

"S-s-sorry about that. Obviously, I'm not ready for prime time behind the wheel. We need to retire this thing before someone gets hurt. But here's the good news—I know what the message means. Where's the guidebook?"

"Can I drive now?" Dan asked again.

"Not a chance."

"Come on! Let me drive! Please!"

Within the space of thirty seconds, Dan asked if he could drive nine more times before finally handing over the guidebook. Amy flipped to Siberia, to a picture she'd seen with a caption that had interested her.

"Okay, check this out. A long time ago, back when they had labor camps in these Siberian outposts, they put a lot of the political prisoners to work on this one road. It was long. I mean *really* long, and it was a grueling job. Sometimes, when prisoners dropped dead on the job, they'd use their bones in the road itself."

"The Road of Bones," said Dan. "That's a little bit unpleasant even by my standards."

"And totally real. See?"

Amy held out the picture, which showed men with shovels and spades standing in the middle of nowhere with a long white road sprawling out behind them.

"Hamilton is going to love this. The Road of Bones! You can't make that sort of thing up."

"The M and the S in the stone, that has to refer to Magadan, Siberia. It's one of the three places we have left to go."

"And the arrow points away, toward the pile of bones. So if someone were to start in Magadan and drive, what, fifty-two miles down the Road of Bones, they might find something?"

"Precisely," said Amy.

Dan held the stone in the light once more and looked at all the parts inscribed. It added up. Broken bones, the number fifty-two, the arrow pointing away from M, S.

"We better call Hamilton," said Dan.

Amy dialed Nellie's cell phone and hoped Hamilton would be standing by, not goofing off or having a big brawl with the Kabras. He answered on the first ring.

"That you, Amy?" Hamilton answered. "I hope you have something for us to do. My dad is getting so bored he's throwing rocks at the birds. He thinks we're on a wild goose chase."

"Not even close!" said Amy. "And you're doing a great job. We've got to get you to Magadan as fast as we can."

"Well, then, you're in luck," said Hamilton.

"What do you mean?"

"We had to clear out of Omsk. That place was un-Holt friendly in the extreme. So I figured what the heck, chances are I'm probably needed in Magadan next anyway. It was the only other place you gave me to go. We hopped a plane last night and we're already here. The Kabras followed us, though. Those guys are like a wad of gum on your shoe. They keep getting a free ride."

"Hamilton! You're a genius!" said Amy.

"Finally someone noticed."

Amy put Hamilton on the speakerphone.

"So where am I going? Give me the news," Hamilton said.

Dan did the honors, after which Hamilton just about blew a gasket.

"No way! This thing is real? The Road of Bones? Sweet! Dan, you are SO jealous. Don't even pretend like you're not."

Dan was so frustrated he wanted to jump out of his underwear. He couldn't drive Tiny Tim, he couldn't go to the Road of Bones. He was being iced out!

"Get to work, Hamilton," said Amy. "We'll be standing by for your next lead. And don't take the Kabras lightly. They're ruthless—they'll do anything to stop you."

"The Hammer is on the job. I'll be back in touch." The line went dead.

Dan stewed in the front seat while Amy tried to get up enough nerve to start Tiny Tim again. They were either going to Moscow or Yekaterinburg. Either way, they were getting very close to the end of the hunt, and not a minute too soon. The clock was down to eight hours and counting.

Amy jumped as the phone vibrated in her hand. *Number unknown.*

"Hello?"

"Hi, Amy. It's Ian. Been thinking about me?"

Ian with the silky voice that sent chills down her spine.

"What do *you* want? Wait — how did you get this number?"

"I'm worried about you. You're in way over your head, love. You should be careful who you trust."

"I can check you and your sister off my list! And don't call me love!"

"Look, Amy, I've been trying to play nice. You and Dan are fun to chase, but there's something you should know."

"What's that?" said Amy. She covered the mouth-piece and told Dan who it was. Dan stuck his finger down his throat and started fake puking.

"You're hopelessly behind," said Ian. "I don't want to hurt your feelings, but lots of clues have already been found, including the one you're looking for."

"You're lying!" said Amy. "You don't even know where we're going. Yeah, I know all about it. You're stuck out in Siberia somewhere. Well, here's a little sur-prise for you, Ian. You're three thousand miles from where you need to be."

There was a slight pause on the line, then a classic Kabra laugh, sly and almost imperceptible.

"Oh, Amy. If only you knew the truth. You can't say I didn't warn you."

The phone clicked off, and Amy started up Tiny Tim. She was so angry she jammed on the gas and spun the tires, her fear of driving a distant memory.

"He's lying. They don't have any more clues than we do, right, Dan?"

But Dan wouldn't meet her eyes. For the rest of the drive they were both completely silent.

CHAPTER 10

"This way," whispered Reagan Holt, "stay low or they'll see us coming."

Against all his natural tendencies, Eisenhower Holt crept along as quietly as a mouse. His huge frame was much more suited to tackling someone from behind and beating the tar out of him.

"Do you see anyone?" he asked.

"No. I think they went this way."

Reagan was peering around the corner of an aqua concrete building that hadn't seen a fresh coat of paint in fifty years. She and her father were tracking two people down a potholed street lined with decaying buildings.

"Where did they go?" boomed Eisenhower Holt. "They're like cats, those two!"

"Dad, will you *please* keep it down? Don't you know the meaning of the word *whisper*?"

Eisenhower Holt was about to retort when he and Reagan were jumped from behind. The bigger of the two attackers landed on Eisenhower's back, put an arm around his neck, and wouldn't let go. Reagan and a smaller assailant rolled around in the dirt while Eisenhower spun in a great circle, his captor's legs swinging in the air behind him.

"Sneak attack! I told you to zip it!" yelled Reagan. She was in a serious fight, punching and kicking from below a girl her exact same size.

"I'll save you!" said Eisenhower.

"Too late," said the person on his back. "I got it!"

"And that's the game!" said Mary-Todd, throwing her hands up as she appeared from out of nowhere. "This round goes to Hamilton and Madison. Nice job on the switchback."

Mary-Todd Holt pulled out a well-worn pocket-size journal and made a notation.

"You're falling behind in the standings, sugar maple. You can do better."

Eisenhower had flopped down on all fours, his usual move when he'd lost the flag. Hamilton, Reagan, and Madison jumped on board. When Eisenhower stood up again, he shook with all his might until his children fell off in a pile at his feet.

"I keep telling you," fumed Reagan, "you need to be quieter. We'll never catch up if you can't learn to stalk like a cat."

"Look at the size of these guns!" yelled Eisenhower, pointing to his preposterously bulging biceps. "It ain't easy keeping these guys still. They like to fight."

"My dad is a dork," said Reagan. "Someone help me, please."

Eisenhower pulled Hamilton aside, threw an arm around him, and began walking. The father and son were like two buildings, big and solid.

"Did you hear from them yet?" asked Eisenhower. He knew it was past time for a father-son chat, but somehow they never went quite as planned.

"Just a few minutes ago," said Hamilton. Already the boy was looking defensive. "They told me where to go. I think we're getting close."

"We're putting an awful lot of trust in you on this deal. It would be a monumental disappointment if they were tricking us."

"No way, Dad. This is the real deal. I'm sure of it."

"You better be. You fail, the whole family fails. And you know how I feel about failure."

They walked a little farther and Eisenhower slapped his son on the back.

"You do realize we'll have to double-cross them in the end. We can't risk falling behind here. If a clue comes our way, we need to keep it for ourselves. And don't think for a second they won't do the same to us given the chance. They're no better than their parents were in that department."

"Dad . . . I was thinking. We've got a lot more stuff to find before this is over," said Hamilton, tension visible in his shoulders. "Maybe a partnership makes sense?"

"You going soft on me?" asked Eisenhower. "This is a competition, not a playdate. When the time comes, we cut the cord and leave them behind. End of discussion."

"But, Dad—"

"I said END OF DISCUSSION! Don't overstep your pay grade, young man. Just get the job done and leave the rest to me."

Hamilton's shoulders slumped, and deep in Eisenhower's chest, his heart squeezed. But there was a chain of command that had to be followed. Or else people got hurt. Even killed.

"My dad was bigger than me," said Eisenhower, his eyes on his own family. "A mountain of a man."

Eisenhower fell silent as they walked back toward the twins, thinking about his father. Eisenhower's mother had died really young and it had been just the two guys living together. A lot of sports. Not a lot of anything else. And that had been fine. Just *fine*.

"Fall in, team!" cried Eisenhower. "New orders!"

"We can't seem to shake those Kabras," said Mary-Todd, thumbing her hand behind her. A black Land Rover had pulled into an alley, where it sat idling, spewing exhaust.

"We'll deal with them soon enough," said Eisenhower. He looked at his son with a mix of admiration and concern, which was the closest thing to praise he knew how to give.

"Tell us where we're going, Ham. And make it snappy!"

"I have a hunch about something else," said Amy. "Do you want to hear it?"

They were sitting in the St. Petersburg airport, awaiting instructions, and Dan was itching to hit the magazine stand for some junk food.

"Can it wait until I refill the backpack with provisions?"

Amy rolled her eyes.

As they walked, Amy laid out her idea. "Everything we've found has been carved or sculpted, right? First it was the little room in the paperweight, then the Rasputin figurine, then the coat of arms carved into wood and painted, and finally the stone with the broken bones. They're all intricately made pieces of art."

They entered the store and Dan started perusing the shelves.

"And we keep getting this recurring color—orange, like honey," said Amy. "The paperweight was a murky orange. Rasputin's model, it's the same. The snake was orange, the stone is orange. At first I thought it was just a Russian thing, but I'm starting to think it means something else."

"Uh-huh," said Dan, barely paying attention as he grabbed a handful of candy bars. "So what's it mean?"

His arms were overflowing with bags of chips, gum, and candy, which he dumped onto the counter.

Amy leaned in to whisper, "I think when NRR talks about 'the room,' he's talking about the Amber Room."

"What's that?" asked Dan.

"Nine hundred rubles," said the lady at the cash register.

They paid, dropped most of the snacks in the backpack, and continued walking. Amy started into a chocolate square while Dan devoured a Kit Kat bar. "It's a room made out of amber."

Dan looked blank, so Amy continued. "You know, that stuff they got the dinosaur DNA from in *Jurassic Park*. This room was absolutely amazing. Wall after wall of intricately carved images. It's a priceless treasure. And guess where it was? At Catherine Palace in the royal village."

Half the Whoppers crammed into Dan's mouth sprayed out. "We were just there! Why didn't you tell me? We could have stopped in and found something important."

"It would have been a waste of time. The Amber Room was stolen by the Nazis in World War Two. And then it disappeared. No one knows where it ended up, but some think it secretly made its way back into Russia after the war."

"How do you lose a *room*?"

"It's over a hundred and fifty feet of walls, to be precise. And they used six tons of amber," said Amy, switching over to the bossy teacher voice that grated on Dan's ears.

"I'm guessing the Amber Room, if that really is the room we're after, is either in Moscow or Yakville," said Dan.

"Yekaterinburg," corrected Amy, popping another square of chocolate into her mouth.

"Whatever. Let's just hope it's not in Siberia with the Holts."

Bzzzzzzzzzz. Bzzzzzzzzzz. Bzzzzzzzzzz.

Amy and Dan had both fallen asleep in the airport while Nellie's phone vibrated. On the fourth vibration, Dan woke up. The phone sat between them on the backpack.

"Hello? That you, Hamilton?"

"Wooooooohoooooooo!" sounded a voice from the other end. Dan held the phone away from his ear and Amy stirred awake, rubbing her eyes.

"We fell asleep," she said.

"No, duh," said Dan. "I think I've got Hammerhead on the line. He's in high spirits."

"Hamilton here! My dad just took the wheel. We're taking turns with this thing. It's amazing!"

"What are you talking about?" said Dan.

"Dude, we're driving a KAMAZ truck down the Road of Bones! This thing is like a tank!"

"NO WAY!" howled Dan. "A KAMAZ truck? Are you kidding? That's a classic!"

"What's a KAMAZ truck?" asked Amy, listening in.

"It's the Godzilla of all Hummers! The Russian Monster Truck! Plus, it's a Transformer . . . sort of . . . I mean, they use the same giant mother of a chassis and build a monster anything on top—dump trucks, army trucks, all-terrain buses—the KAMAZ is an all-weather, twelve-gear hunk of metal! How could you not know about this?!"

"Okaaaaaaaaaay," said Amy.

"That should be me driving!" Dan yelled into the phone.

"Eat your heart out," said Hamilton.

Amy grabbed the phone. "What's going on? Where are you?"

"We're heading back. Already made it to mile fifty-two WAY ahead of the Kabras. They bottomed out ten miles back. Reagan wanted to help 'em out when we passed by, but Dad said, 'Let 'em call a tow truck.' Dude! It's a KAMAZ!"

Dan plugged his ears. He couldn't stand the sound of Hamilton Holt having so much fun while he sat bored in an airport. Amy grabbed the phone.

"What did you find? Hamilton? Are you there?"

The line was loaded with static, cutting in and out as the truck passed over the Road of Bones.

"Hamilton, listen to me. I can barely hear you. What did you find? We're running out of time here!"

"Oh, yeah, I almost forgot! It wasn't hard to see once we got there, I'll tell you that. The thing was just sitting there on the side of the road."

Dan could tell Amy was about to blow a gasket while Hamilton stalled.

"WHAT was sitting on the side of the road?"

"Uh-oh," said Hamilton. "There's the Kabras. They are NOT happy. What the—? No way!"

A loud crunching noise filled the cell phone speaker. Even Dan could hear it.

"My dad just drove over the Land Rover! This is incredible! You GOTTA try this! What's . . . oh, no . . . hey!"

"WHAT . . . DID . . . YOU . . . FIND?" Amy yelled. She looked at Dan. "What's oh, no? Why the oh, no?"

The line crackled and popped, then Mary-Todd Holt got on the line.

"Hello, Amy, how are you? Hamilton and his father are . . . well they're having a little skirmish with a couple of very big—oh, my, that had to hurt—PUNCH HIM BACK, EISENHOWER! . . . Sorry, dear. I can tell you what we found. There was a stake in the ground on the side of the road at mile marker fifty-two. It was in there really deep, but my strongman Mr. Holt got it out. Yanked it until his back seized up—that's why

Hamilton got to drive the truck. They've been taking turns. Anyway, it was attached to the strangest thing. The bottom wasn't what you'd think, like a big block of concrete, it was a—well . . . it was a head. Not a real one, mind you—wouldn't that be unpleasant?—I mean it was a sculpted head—NICE SHOT, HAMILTON! SHOW 'EM WHAT YOU GOT!—Pardon me, but my boy just clobbered one of these bodyguards right over the head with . . . um . . . *the head.* He's doing a fine job out there. Where was I? Oh, yes, the head. It appears I'm going to have to get back to you on that. GET 'EM, HOLTS! HIT 'EM WHERE IT HURTS!"

The line went dead.

"You have *got* to be kidding me," said Amy.

Four minutes passed before the phone buzzed back to life.

"We got 'em on the run!"

It was Dan who picked up, and this time Hamilton was calling.

"My dad is hobbled," said Hamilton. "But he's as tough as they come. Mom and the twins are out there bringing him in. Listen, I'm about to go a little rogue here. My dad's not too big on me telling you what we found. Dude, can I trust you? I mean *really* trust you? If you double-cross me, my dad will go totally ballistic."

"You can trust me—I promise."

And the funny thing was, Dan was telling the truth. Something in his gut told him he wouldn't be able to hold out after Hamilton had helped them so much.

"Here's the deal," Hamilton started. "I'm no history nerd, but I know this head. Even my dad knew this head, after being here for awhile. It's that Lenin guy, the one who started the Russian Revolution."

"The guy with the pointy goatee?"

Hamilton started in about the driving and the cool head again, but he didn't have long before Amy ripped the phone out of Dan's hand.

"Fork over the information, Hamilton! We're running out of time!"

"Oh, great," Hamilton groaned. "It's the bossy one. Get a pen and I'll tell you what's written across Lenin's head."

"I'm ready," said Amy, already poised with a pad and pencil, ready to write down whatever came out of Hamilton's mouth.

"SKP BAL BOX4 R3 D1 45231 D2 45102 D3 NRR."

"Are you sure you got it right?" asked Amy.

"It's right! Stop bugging me. What do we do now?"

Amy looked at Dan, who shrugged.

"Um . . . you've done a great job helping us. Head back to Moscow. We'll be in touch as soon as we know something."

"Over and out," said Hamilton.

Amy turned to Dan.

"Are you ready? You and I are going to break into the Kremlin."

CHAPTER 11

Ian Kabra couldn't decide what was worse: being stranded on a road of bones, or having to put up with his little sister.

"Look at me! This is a disaster!" she howled.

Ian quirked his lip at that. Natalie's leggings were torn, her Prada shoes were scuffed beyond repair, and her normally sleek hair looked like it had been gone over with an eggbeater. Ian knew he hadn't fared much better, bruised and battered after an all-out rumble with the Holts.

"This clue hunt is stupid. Stupid! Stupid! *Stupid!*" Natalie said, her voice particularly shrill in the small backseat of the busted-up Land Rover. The driver was on the phone trying to reach a tow company and gingerly feeling his broken nose.

"The big guy is quicker than he looks," said Ian, trying to lighten the mood. "I'd hate to take him on when his back is working properly."

"Face it, Ian, we've hit bottom. They trashed the car. We're sitting on a road of *peasant bones,* and we're stuck in Siberia. It's a nightmare. I WANT TO GO HOME!"

That was it. Ian couldn't take one more second confined in a small space with Natalie. He stepped out of the car and paced, dialing his phone. Five rings later, he hung up, unable to reach his father. *As usual.* He dialed again. This time, after three rings, Irina Spasky answered.

"I'm busy," she snapped.

"Our day isn't going as well as I'd expected. I hope you have better news for me."

"Couldn't handle the Holts? Why am I not surprised?"

Ian refused to be distracted by the sniping. He gathered himself, took a very deep breath, and put in the order.

"You have to get rid of them. They're working with the Holts, and I'm pretty certain they've relayed another message. Dan and Amy are too close."

For some reason, Amy's face and her stupid stutter flashed into his mind. He paused. "Get them out of Russia."

He had chosen his words carefully. It was not officially a kill order. And yet he knew Irina would go to any extreme to remove the risk.

"Agreed," Irina finally answered.

"Relay the details when you've accomplished your task."

Irina clicked off her phone.

It was done.

The one-hour flight from St. Petersburg to Moscow gave Amy and Dan the time they needed to decipher the riddle and formulate a plan. They were back in their disguises, and this time they decided to leave them on until they were finished exploring the Kremlin. It didn't seem like a good idea to visit the Russian center of power looking like two kids who'd gotten separated from their parents.

Lenin, Amy had immediately assumed, was a reference to the Kremlin, where the preserved body of the leader of the Russian Revolution was still on display, decades after his death.

This time, the rest of the riddle required the skills of both Dan and Amy. Amy was quick to put the first part together: SKP, she was sure, stood for State Kremlin Palace, a prestigious concert hall on the sprawling grounds of the Kremlin. Dan was first to suggest the meaning of the rest of the numbers and letters.

"BAL BOX4 R3 must be a row of seats. Balcony Box Four, third row, to be exact," Dan said.

Amy nodded approvingly. "I don't *always* think you were switched at birth with my real brother. The rest of the numbers must be some sort of combination or code. I bet we can figure it out when we get there."

A dash through the airport and a quick cab ride later, Dan and Amy stood squarely in front of the State Kremlin Palace, the guidebook open. They were down to a couple of hours, and a sense of heightened urgency crackled in their voices.

"We'll need to get to the upper section," said Amy. They were looking at a seating chart for the State Kremlin Palace, where Amy had circled Row 3 in one of the balcony boxes.

Amy checked her watch again.

"Two hours and counting. I don't think we're going to make it."

"We'll make it," said Dan, heading for the entrance of the looming white theater.

There was a hallway outside the main seating area, with doors leading inside and lots of ornate artwork on the walls. Tourists were perusing the space, waiting for a chance to get inside and look around. The next tour didn't start for another twenty minutes.

"This is our chance," whispered Amy. "Come on, we'll sneak in while everyone is milling around."

Somewhere in the deep recesses of the very building in which Dan and Amy searched, a person tracked their every move.

Very resourceful, these two, NRR thought. *They might make the deadline after all.*

NRR dialed a phone and let it ring several times before the call was picked up.

"Is this a secure line?"

"I will not dignify that with an answer," NRR answered.

"Okay, okay. Just make it quick."

"I will be seeing them shortly. Do you still want me to go through with it?"

A pause ensued on the line. NRR was used to this. The contact was a thinker who liked to weigh every option.

"They are extraordinary, aren't they? No one can say they haven't proven themselves."

"They understood from the start it could not be done alone," NRR responded.

"And recruiting a team like the Holts? Simply remarkable. I didn't think it was possible."

"So we go ahead, then?" asked NRR.

"We're a go. If they make it to your desk, take them to the room. I think they're ready."

The line went dead and NRR turned back to the bank of video screens.

CHAPTER 12

All the doors into the theater were locked, but it was only a few minutes before a maintenance worker emerged, pushing a garbage can on wheels. Dan saw the opportunity they needed and shoved Amy into the man's path. When she hit the cart, Amy caught her foot on the metal wheel and flew forward onto the marble floor.

"You little monster!" she said, turning beet red and forgetting for a moment that she was visiting one of the more opulent concert halls in Europe, disguised as an adult.

When she got up, the man was wearing a cramped smile, trying not to laugh. He mumbled something in Russian that Amy felt sure meant "hopeless klutz," then wandered down the long corridor, shaking his head.

"Dan?"

Amy looked every which way, straightening her ridiculous wig and glasses, but there was no sign of her brother.

"Pssst. Over here," said Dan.

Amy turned around and saw that a door to the theater was open just far enough for Dan's goatee to poke out at her.

"Get in here before someone sees you."

Amy backed up slowly as a group of women walked past, chatting quietly in Russian. By the time they'd disappeared, Amy had her back against one of the two doors. Dan grabbed her by the arm and yanked her inside.

"What's taking you so long?"

Amy scowled at her brother. *First he pushes me, then he pulls me. Now he gets all over my case.*

"You're starting to annoy me," she said, gearing up for an epic brother-sister argument. But when she turned toward the stage, her anger melted away. Amy loved the theater almost as much as she loved books, and the State Kremlin Palace was a stunner if ever she'd seen one. The stage was set with blue lights shining down as night descended on the scene. There were scale model buildings and a Russian-style church deep in the background. It was breathtaking from where they stood, like a scene from a fairy tale in which Anastasia came back to life and Rasputin roamed the woods.

Long rows of seats lined the middle of the theater, all of them empty, awaiting theatergoers who wouldn't arrive until evening.

Dan led the way into the darkness along the back wall of the theater. "The balcony's up there, so the stairs can't be too far. This place is gigantic. It must hold at least six thousand people."

They could hear a door opening as they crept onto the stairs, which were hidden behind a curtain. Amy put her finger to her lips, then looked back to see that a security guard had entered. And what was worse, he had a giant German shepherd on a leash.

Dan waved Amy along and soon they were at the top of the gilded stairway, down a short hall, and standing in Balcony Box 4. Dan began searching for row number 3, then tried to imagine what D1 meant. He hadn't got that far in his thinking before Amy could tell he was stumped. She crouched down low, peering over the edge of the balcony. The dog was guiding the guard closer toward the stairs.

"He's coming this way!" said Amy.

She crept over to Dan, and they both looked at the scribble of numbers and letters on the piece of paper again.

"There are three Ds — D1, D2, D3. Maybe they refer to doors?"

"Could be," said Dan. He whispered all the letters and numbers again. Sometimes it helped to say things out loud. "SKP BAL BOX4 R3 D1 45231 D2 45102 D3 NRR."

"Hurry, Dan! That dog is serious business. It looks angry *and* hungry. You know what that means—"

Dan walked along Row 3 and sat down.

"What are you doing? This is no time to sit around! Do something!"

"I am," said Dan. "I think I got this."

"You think you got *what*?" Amy said nervously. She was searching on the floor for a button or a lock, anything that might get them away from the approaching guard dog. "Look for some dials or a hidden panel. Make yourself useful!"

Dan calmly got up and sat in the next seat over, seat number 5 in the row. He'd been in seat number 4. Then he got up again and sat in seat number 2.

"Seriously, Dan, you've lost your marbles."

"I don't think so," he whispered. "45231 might be the order in which a person has to sit in the seats in Row 3. Let me finish."

He sat in seat number 3, then moved right up next to Amy.

"If something doesn't happen when I sit down, we're in big trouble."

He took a deep breath and plopped down in the seat. There was a soft *snick* behind a curtained wall at the rear of the balcony.

"I think you did something," whispered Amy. She could hear the German shepherd sniffing at the top of the stairs now.

Dan and Amy moved quietly to the rear of the balcony and pulled back the red curtain. One of the panels had slid open an inch, revealing a black seam of darkness behind.

"Kto tam?"

Amy nearly jumped out of the balcony at the sound of the guard's voice. He was right outside, about to enter, as Dan slid the panel open just enough to glide through. Amy followed and the curtain dropped. She slid the panel shut.

The German shepherd whined and sniffed, searching everything in the balcony, including the curtain. But the dog didn't find anything. Dan and Amy had vanished.

"I guess we follow the lights," said Amy.

They were in a long, narrow corridor with runway lights embedded in the center of the floor. The walls and ceiling were black, so that it felt like walking in the midnight sky along a line of stars. They snaked back and forth for fifty feet and came to the end.

"Looks like an elevator," said Dan. "D2 — door number two."

Amy nodded her agreement in the darkness. A row of five elevator buttons, each round and circled in red, glowed softly against the black wall.

"Remember the order?" asked Amy. Dan stepped up to the bank of buttons and began pushing them one at a time. First the 4, then the 5, then the 1, 0, and 2.

The doors opened with surprising speed and Dan jumped back, accidentally clocking Amy in the arm with his elbow. The entire back wall of the elevator was covered with a giant portrait of the Kabra family. Ian looked particularly smug.

"They really think a lot of themselves, don't they?" said Dan.

"You said it," agreed Amy.

They glanced at each other, and Dan could see that Amy's hands were trembling again. She had a lot on her plate, being the older of the two, always having to be the responsible one. Dan felt an unexpected twinge of guilt. "We're doing okay, you know," he said.

Amy started to smile, but just then the elevator began to plummet. She grabbed a rail and held on for dear life. Dan wasn't so lucky. He rolled around on the floor of the elevator until it came to an abrupt stop, the doors opening once more.

"I'm starting to think this place is haunted," said Dan. There was something about being way underground that scared Dan, like he was trapped in a mine shaft and the air was running out. "How far belowground do you think we are?"

Amy didn't answer. Her eyes were locked on the monstrous Gothic door that stood twenty feet in front of them down a cavelike passageway.

"This is *so* Dungeons and Dragons," said Dan.

"It's D3, the last door. Dan, I think we found him. We found NRR."

"We've discovered a lot more than that. I think we just found some sort of old stronghold."

Amy walked out of the elevator and Dan followed until they stood before a door of iron and wood with an ancient set of dials set into its surface. There was only one problem. The writing on the dials was in Russian.

"Give me the guidebook," said Amy. Dan unzipped the backpack and handed the book to Amy. She thumbed through the pages, trying to remember. . . .

"Here! This is it. It's zero to ten written out in Russian and English."

Dan leaned over and glanced at the page. The passage was dimly lit at best, but he could see the strange Russian letters.

"Are we sure about this?" asked Dan.

Everything about their Russian journey had smelled like a trap, and now they'd entered some sort of secret lair from which they might not be able to escape. But none of that mattered to Amy, and she was pretty sure it didn't matter to Dan, either. *Come alone, as your parents did.* The words thrummed in her mind, driving her forward.

"What if Mom and Dad were here?" she whispered. "They could have stood right here, trying to figure this out. It's like they're calling us."

Dan nodded.

"That's exactly how I feel," he said.

"You want to do the honors?" asked Amy.

"You bet I do," said Dan. He scanned the list for a few seconds and went to work on the dials.

"Four . . . Five . . . One . . . Zero . . . Two."

When the last dial was turned, the lock clicked open and the door slid back on its hinges with a grinding sound of old metal. A female voice echoed quietly from behind the door.

"Come in. I have been expecting you."

CHAPTER 13

"This place gives me the serious creeps," Dan whispered.

"You're not k-k-kidding," stammered Amy. No one was waiting for them. They'd entered a small, round room with an elaborate painting that covered all the walls and the domed ceiling. There were no doors except the one that had closed behind them.

"Where'd she go?" asked Dan. "And how the heck are we getting out of here?"

Amy shrugged her shoulders nervously, gazing at the intricately painted walls around her.

"It looks like something Michelangelo would have done."

"Hey!" said Dan. "I know some of these people. That's Ben Franklin!"

Sure enough, the bespectacled figure was towering over their heads, holding the string for a kite and smiling into the sky.

"And I'm pretty sure that's Napoleon. He's definitely small enough," said Amy.

"That's gotta be Churchill," said Dan, spying a round man making the V sign.

"Dan," said Amy, her eyes huge in her face. "They're all Lucians. Every one of them."

Dan's stomach sank. It could only mean one thing. "We're in a Lucian stronghold," he whispered.

"Bad," said Amy. "Very bad! Let's get out of here!"

She ran her hands frantically over the great surface of the door, searching for a latch or a dial that would set them free.

"Come on, Dan!"

There was a fast sliding sound from one of the walls, and Dan turned around to see that a panel on the far wall had opened. The painted form of Sir Isaac Newton stood next to the door and seemed to beckon them forward.

The voice returned, confident and smooth as silk.

"There is no need to be afraid. Follow the lights. Quickly now, before you're caught!"

A runway of lights directed them down an endless hall, just as they had upstairs. These lights were orange, not white as the others had been, and they seemed to go on forever.

"Follow the lights until you reach the twelfth door on the left. And hurry! These halls never stay empty for long."

"The voice must be coming from a speaker in this room," said Amy. "She's not in here."

Dan and Amy took one last look at each other and nodded. They had no choice. Not two steps in, the panel slid shut and it was more dark than light.

"How many doors is that?" said Dan, trying to figure out just how imprisoned they'd become. "We're *never* getting out of here."

They counted the doors until at last they came to the twelfth. They stood for a long, silent moment. A door opened somewhere in the distance and they stood perfectly still. Dan turned his head and saw a figure seven or eight doors back walking away. The panel opened just long enough for the person to slip through and then it closed again.

"An agent of some k-k-kind, no doubt," whispered Amy.

"Let's do this," said Dan.

He lifted his hand to the knob, then hesitated.

"Are you absolutely sure we went twelve doors on the left side?" asked Dan. "It would be a real bummer if we were knocking on the wrong door."

The last thing Dan wanted to do was barge in on a meeting between dark-suited secret agents.

Amy hesitated. Dan could tell she wanted to go back and recount, just to be sure, but the panel at the far end of the hall opened again.

Dan turned the knob and the two of them darted inside the room, slamming the door behind them.

They were in what appeared to be a rather run-of-the-mill office. There was a big oak desk, a rug over a wooden floor, and a freestanding globe of the world. A long white coat hung on an equally white coatrack, and the Lucian crest filled one entire wall. The only thing at all remarkable about the room was the person sitting behind the desk.

She wore a suit of white, which was all the more striking against her black hair. And she was, in a word, ageless. Dan couldn't have said whether she was forty or sixty, for there was something very old about her eyes, and yet her face was unlined. She was beautiful in a classic Russian way. Amy stared at her as if the woman were a queen.

"You do make things interesting. I like that about you. Please, come, sit down," the woman said.

There were two chairs before her desk, and Dan and Amy promptly did what they were told.

"You may dispense with the disguises. They do you no good here."

Dan had set the backpack on the floor. He was happy to tear the mustache and goatee off his face and drop them in the backpack, glancing at his watch as he did. *We made it!* he thought. *Only minutes to spare, but Amy and I did it!*

Amy's hair tumbled down as she took off the black wig and dropped it in the backpack.

"You're very pretty, young lady," said the woman in white. "I hope Grace was kind enough to tell you that when she was alive."

"You knew Grace?"

The woman nodded, her eyes brimming with secrets.

"You might say our families go way back. I never met Grace Cahill personally. My mother did. They were both remarkable women—my mother and your grandmother. Remarkable women have a way of finding one another."

I hope this remarkable woman doesn't kill us, thought Dan.

Amy seemed to have no reservations. Her cheeks turned pink and she asked, "Are you the grand duchess Anastasia?"

The moment Amy said the words, NRR burst out laughing.

A light flashed on her desk and she resumed her air of dignity.

"If you'll excuse me a moment," she said. "Very bad timing, but I'm afraid it can't be helped."

She turned in her chair, away from Dan and Amy, and drew open the doors on a wooden credenza to reveal a bank of monitors. One of them was receiving a feed from the painted room Dan and Amy had just left.

"If you would be so kind, could you hide behind the desk? A call is coming in from someone who would find it very curious to see the two of you here."

It was getting stranger by the minute, but Dan and Amy felt they had no choice, so down on the floor they went. A few seconds later, a familiar voice filled the room.

"Hello, Nataliya Ruslanovna Radova. You're looking picture-perfect as usual."

"You're too kind, Irina Nikolaievna Spaskaya. What do you need?"

Dan couldn't believe his ears. Irina Spasky was calling in. Every muscle in his body tensed as it now seemed positive they were trapped.

"I need you to send a team to the room. There's a lot of activity going on and I want to make sure it's well guarded."

"Funny you should call. Ian Kabra made the same request only an hour ago. We're already building a black circle."

"Excellent. Did he tell you he was in Siberia, chasing the Holts down the Road of Bones? He's got himself into quite a mess."

"His father was not pleased, as you might imagine."

"Maybe Vikram will finally come to his senses and put them both back in school, where they belong."

"Would you like me to send the Shark to pick you up?" asked Nataliya.

"That's an excellent idea. I've had some complications of my own, but I think I can get to the room before nightfall. Bring the Shark to me, I'll bring it back. We can have that cup of tea you've been promising me."

"Be careful."

"I'm always careful."

There was a pause in the room and then Nataliya told Amy and Dan they could come out.

"I've never heard Irina so . . . I don't know . . . talkative," said Amy.

"We have been friends a long, long time," said the woman in white. She placed her elbows on the desk. "I understand her, so she talks."

"Let me get one thing straight," said Dan. "Are you NRR?"

The woman in white smiled thinly without showing her teeth. "You were expecting a man, I suppose."

"Uh . . . well . . . not exactly," said Dan. "Okay, you got me. I was expecting a dude."

The woman in white chuckled and shook her head. "I am NRR. Sorry to disappoint you."

Dan tried to offer an apology, but NRR put her hand up so authoritatively it clammed him right up.

"We've got enough time for a few more questions, but the call from Irina changes things. Your access to the room grows perilously small."

"I don't understand," said Amy. She sounded frustrated and maybe even a little bit angry. "Are you a Lucian or not? Why are you helping us? Who are you?"

The woman in white sighed deeply, folded her fingers together, and tried to explain.

"I am not the grand duchess Anastasia, though I must thank you for the compliment. You're not far off the mark. Anastasia Nikolaievna Romanova was my mother."

"Your *mother?!*" said Dan, dumbstruck by what Nataliya was saying. "You're Anastasia's daughter? That's insane!"

"Her only child, yes."

"And she knew Grace Cahill?" asked Amy. "You expect us to believe our grandmother knew the grand duchess Anastasia?"

"Oh, yes, they were quite close, actually. I'm sure you've heard the rumors about my mother. They're true. She was not killed with the rest of her family. She escaped. And as I said, remarkable women have a way of finding one another."

Amy was struck silent, but Dan was happy to fill the void.

"So everything we've imagined actually happened! Rasputin had some serious death-defying ninja skills and he passed them on to Anastasia!"

"Does he always talk this way?" NRR asked Amy, clearly amused.

"He does. It's a problem."

"He'll grow out of it."

Dan's head swiveled back and forth. They had formed some sort of girl alliance! "I'm sitting right here! Stop talking about me," said Dan.

NRR made a calming motion with her hands,

glanced at her watch, and gave Dan and Amy a look that said time was running very short.

"You're a grand duchess, like your mom," said Amy. "Grand Duchess Nataliya."

Dan frowned. Amy looked like she was about to bow or something.

"I'm afraid those days are long gone, Amy. We're not like the British, with their kings and queens. The age of royalty has passed in Russia. But what I do today honors my mother's memory."

"How?" Dan asked. "You want to help us find this secret because . . . ?" He wasn't about to be taken in by this woman just because she was pretty and had an awesome accent. Had James Bond taught him *nothing*?

"What I tell you now must never leave this room. My life and the lives of others would be compromised. You understand?"

Dan and Amy nodded.

"My mother, my grandmother—all of them were Lucians. I, too, am a Lucian. But like so many who are born into one branch or another, most of my family was never actively involved in . . . what is Grace calling it? The clue hunt. In fact, for a very long time, my mother was unaware of her Lucian heritage at all. Then came my father, who my mother met much later in life. He was one of the most powerful Lucians of the past fifty years. Before the Kabras, it was my father in charge. It's why I hold such a sensitive position, why we got involved to begin with. So you see, I am a Lucian, a very power-ful one at that. But I am first and foremost myself."

Nataliya brushed a dark strand of hair away from her face. She was so elegant and poised, but she had inherited that mischievous Anastasia flair Amy had talked so much about.

"Why are you helping us?" Dan persisted. He still didn't understand what Nataliya's story had to do with them. Why would an heir to the Romanov throne care about two kids?

Nataliya looked at her gold watch again, then tapped her desk phone.

"Irina has requested backup. Prepare the Shark for departure in fifteen minutes."

Nataliya turned her gaze to Amy. "I sent you on this chase for many reasons," said Nataliya. "The first was to distract my Lucian counterparts, to confuse them. The Kabras are thousands of miles away in Siberia, and Irina has been frustrated at every turn. Mission accomplished. The second reason was to discover what you are made of. You've been tested all along, no? You knew right away that it would take more than your-selves to find the room. I would never have guessed that *anyone* could bring the Holts under control, but you did it. It is imperative that you learn to work with others to achieve a greater good."

"Okay, so we passed this test and outsmarted the Lucians," said Amy. "I still don't see why you're helping us."

"Or if you're helping us at all," Dan muttered. Nothing Nataliya had said so far led him to believe their dangerous hunt all over Russia would even lead to a Clue.

"I will guide you to what you are looking for," said Nataliya. "Both in this ridiculous contest and beyond." She gave them a meaningful look.

Dan's throat tightened. "You're talking about our parents, aren't you?"

Nataliya tapped an index finger on the desk. She was extremely quiet. It was as if ninety-nine percent of her body had turned to stone, leaving just the finger. Tap, tap, tap.

Finally, after Dan had popped every knuckle on both hands, Nataliya spoke. "Certain information, when you find it, changes you forever. You wish you could go back, but you can't. And still we go searching after secrets. I never wanted any part of this madness about clues, and yet here we all are." She paused. "The Amber Room is hidden in a vault of Lucian secrets. There you will find the Lucian clue and also information about your parents."

Nataliya shook her head. "Grace was very fond of pulling strings, even from the grave. I counsel you to walk away from all this. But if you will not, I will help you. I warn you, you might not thank me for it later."

Nataliya looked at Amy, then turned her mesmerizing eyes to Dan. "I help you because it is what Anastasia Romanova would have wanted. I help you because it is right. But I cannot say if you will like what you find."

Amy was openly crying, and Dan could feel his own eyes fill with tears. It was too much, help that was not help, an ally that fed them riddles and unsavory hints about their parents and Grace. Dan could feel the earth shifting beneath his feet. Again. There was no safe place for them, no one to trust. And no home to go back to.

He looked at Amy and they both nodded.

"We want to go to the Amber Room," said Amy.

Nataliya tipped her head to them and stood up, taking the long white coat in her hand.

"We must hurry, then," she said. "It won't be easy if Irina arrives before you."

Nataliya slid open a desk drawer and removed a small tin canister. Opening it, she took out two small keys and placed them in a pocket of her white coat.

"Do you know where my ancestors were massacred?"

"Yekaterinburg," Amy said. "In a house there."

"Where the Church on the Blood now stands. A terrible name, but sadly appropriate. The church was built much later, but underneath . . . it was there, in the basement, where all of them were shot. Only my mother survived."

"And you're taking us there in this thing called the Shark?" asked Dan, brightening for the first time.

Nataliya went to the door. She opened it and peered down the long, dark hallway.

"The Shark is the quickest way. Now we go."

Dan and Amy followed Nataliya into the hallway. They arrived at an elevator and boarded. Dan had imagined some sort of high-speed watercraft, so he was surprised when the elevator went up instead of down. It opened on the roof of the State Kremlin Palace.

"Here we are," said Nataliya.

"*That's* the Shark?" asked Amy, but Dan was already running toward it.

"It is the fastest helicopter in Russia. She will do three hundred."

The Shark was twice the size of a normal copter, completely black, with a rudder that looked like a shark fin.

"No way!" said Dan. "Three hundred miles per hour? That's, like, a world record!"

"Many world records such as these have long been broken." Nataliya smiled. "We Lucians keep the best toys for ourselves."

Dan ran a circle around the Shark and tried to pry open one of the doors.

"He's excitable, isn't he?" asked Nataliya.

"You don't know the half of it," said Amy.

Nataliya put her arm around Amy and drew her close. "You show great promise. Grace would have been proud of you."

Amy gave her a watery smile.

"Now you must go," Nataliya said.

"What? I don't understand," said Amy. "Aren't you coming with us?"

"I can't."

"But . . . why n-n-not? And how are we supposed to fly this thing? We're not pilots!"

"I will fly you by remote control. I'll get you there safely. But I can't go with you."

"No way!" yelled Dan, bounding over next to them. "It's like the best video game *ever*!"

"I don't understand!" Amy protested.

"If I could, I might hunt the clues myself. But you read about my uncle. You know the struggles he faced."

Amy nodded. Alexei Romanov had been a hemophiliac. The slightest cut would leave him bleeding for weeks.

"I suffer the same fate," said Nataliya. She put her hand in the white pocket and Dan imagined a red stain of blood appearing on Nataliya's snowy jacket.

"A skinned knee or elbow, a bloody nose or a simple cut — if I start bleeding, it doesn't stop. Even with medicine, it's too dangerous for me." Nataliya held out the keys and Amy took them, nodding sadly.

"I'll be in constant communication," said Nataliya. She smiled. "Put on the headphones and get ready for the ride of your life."

It was time to head into the Lucian black circle.

CHAPTER 14

Riding in the Shark made Amy scream with terror. Dan, she assumed, was screaming with joy.

"Wait until Hamilton hears about this! It's untoppable!"

The Shark was stunningly loud at top speed, and Nataliya was pushing it as fast as it would go from her location beneath the Kremlin.

"I love flying the Shark," Amy heard Nataliya say into her headset.

"But you're not really flying it," yelled Amy, trying to be heard over the sound of the blades. It was a scary sensation, flying in a helicopter without a pilot.

"You don't have to yell, I can hear you perfectly," said Nataliya. "From where I'm sitting I might as well be flying the Shark. My control room for the Shark is quite amazing. It's a replica down to the leather on the seats, with wraparound monitors on every side. Front, back, bottom, top—it looks and feels as if I'm really flying the Shark. The only thing missing is the wind and the noise."

"You're lucky," said Amy. "It's rough up here, and loud, and s-s-scary."

"No need to be the slightest bit afraid, Amy. The Shark knows I am its boss."

"What's up, sis?" screamed Dan, bouncing up and down in his seat. "No throwing up in the Shark or we throw you overboard!"

"Close your eyes," said Nataliya. Amy obeyed and tried to calm down while Nataliya spoke softly to her.

"I rarely leave the Lucian surveillance center. It's like being trapped underground, but flying the Shark feels like I've escaped my cage. I've never been to where you'll be going tonight. I've only heard about it. You're going to the place where my ancestors were gunned down in the upheaval of history. What you find there, I fear, will not be pretty."

Nataliya fell silent, letting the words sink in as Amy tried to keep from getting sick.

"I read all about the Amber Room," said Amy. "Can you believe it's been hidden here in Russia all along? There are a lot of people searching for it."

"We Lucians are good at hiding things. And now we've put a black circle around the Church on the Blood.'"

"What's a black circle?"

"It means no Lucians except those given direct permission expressly from Vikram Kabra are allowed to enter."

"How will we know what to look for?" asked Amy.

"There is but one clock inside the room. Set the time for midnight, then one, then midnight again. The face of the clock will open."

"I can remember that."

"You're a smart girl. I'm sure you can."

The rest of the trip passed in silence as everyone watched the sun setting in the western sky. The closer it came to the horizon, the faster Nataliya pushed the Shark toward the Church on the Blood. The noise in the cockpit became almost deafening as the great helicopter struggled to maintain speeds approaching three hundred miles per hour.

The church was located on a small hill of grass in an otherwise sleepy section of town. At this hour, there were few people walking and even fewer cars to contend with. Nataliya announced that given the lateness of their arrival, she would land them directly in front of the church itself. It would be quite a spectacle, but at least there wouldn't be very many people to see it.

"We may be too late," Nataliya said into her microphone. "There's a door in the floor between your feet. You and your brother, get in there and hide. Quickly!"

They were over the church now, descending toward the empty parking lot as the darkness approached.

"You'll need to enter the church through the door at the back using the gold key. Once inside, look for the trail of amber on the floor. The orange key will reveal a set of seven dials. Set them all to amber, with alternating diamonds and hearts. This will open the last door and you'll be inside. Don't be alarmed by what you see. As I have been told, you must first pass through the tomb. Beyond the tomb you'll find the Amber Room."

Dan and Amy didn't comment on what had just been said. There was only one tomb Nataliya could be referring to, the resting place of the six executed Romanovs. Amy's guidebook said they had been moved to the Peter and Paul Cathedral in St. Petersburg. But the Lucians were powerful, especially in Russia. They must have decided to honor their dead more privately.

"Do you see Irina anywhere?" asked Dan.

"The monitors don't show anything," said Nataliya. "But that doesn't mean she isn't here. Irina isn't the type to stand in plain view."

"We're getting inside the hatch," yelled Dan.

"You'll find a flashlight you can use," said Nataliya. "But don't turn it on until you're under the church or someone might see you. There's a monitor down there. Turn it on and you'll see the parking lot. Keep an eye out for a moment when you can escape. Good luck!"

Nothing more could be heard above the noise of the massive black propeller as the Shark came down.

Night had arrived at the Church on the Blood.

"Set a perimeter at a quarter of a mile, Braslov," Nataliya said. She had called Braslov, a surveillance technician who worked three doors down from her own, in the Lucian headquarters. "I've come in a little fast and landed in the parking lot of the church."

"So I noticed," Braslov answered. "I already made the calls."

Nataliya was so immersed in the images of the Church on the Blood she couldn't help feeling like she was sitting in the Shark instead of the safety of a Lucian stronghold.

"Irina saw you and contacted me a few minutes ago," Braslov continued. "The area will be secured."

"Thank you, Braslov."

"You're in the hottest Lucian spot on earth. Don't get burned."

The lights of an approaching police car came into view even before Braslov was through warning Nataliya. A second car followed. The Lucians controlled every level of security in Russia. The agents were fond of sitting around a big table at the Lucian headquarters, coming up with reasons for keeping people out of sensitive areas. The most effective tended to be hazardous spill alerts, which kept people out of designated areas and were often used in black circle situations. They'd been even more careful than usual with the Church on the Blood, which they had just designated a radioactive zone. The police cars were a backup, just in case anyone was curious enough to take a closer look at a giant helicopter.

Nataliya panned her cameras around the lot and saw the dark figure of Irina emerge from a stand of trees. She walked with a stiff confidence, hands in her coat pockets, a woman in charge of her surroundings. A moment later, Irina was standing at the cockpit door, staring into the dark interior of the Shark.

"You couldn't land somewhere a little less conspicuous?" asked Irina. "This kind of event makes problems for us."

Anyone else would have thought Irina was talking to herself, but Nataliya heard the message loud and clear.

"I apologize, Irina. But I thought it was necessary to get here as quickly as possible. I've never pushed the Shark quite so hard."

"She is a lovely beast, no? I look forward to flying her again."

Nataliya watched as Irina peered into the Shark, then back at the church.

"Why so focused on two American brats?" asked Nataliya. "They seem hardly a threat. I've been tracking them from the start, just like all the other teams, and I don't see anything special. They're hopelessly behind."

"Don't underestimate them," said Irina. "They've outsmarted me before."

Irina turned back toward the Shark.

"Let me have a look inside. I haven't taken her for a ride in months."

Nataliya knew all too well how keen Irina's senses were. The slightest mistake on the children's part might lead to disaster. She pressed a white button and the cockpit door unlocked. Then she watched as Irina pulled open the door.

"Keep an eye out with all those cameras of yours, won't you?" said Irina.

"Absolutely."

Nataliya switched to the inside camera and watched as Irina studied the inside of the Shark for anything suspicious. Everything appeared to be in order, so she moved to the back and examined the seats. Still nothing.

"I hope I didn't break something," said Nataliya. "I pushed the Shark getting here so fast."

Without warning, Irina disappeared from view. Nataliya swung the inside camera from side to side, then down to the floor, where she saw Irina lifting the trapdoor. Nataliya's heart thrummed like a hummingbird. *It's over! We're caught!*

But nothing happened. Irina dropped the trapdoor and stepped out of the Shark without a word.

"I'm going inside. You keep a watch out here."

Nataliya breathed a short-lived sigh of relief. At least Dan and Amy hadn't been discovered. She could only assume they'd used what little time they'd had to escape into the church unseen. But they were anything but safe.

Irina Spasky was about to join them in the Church on the Blood.

CHAPTER 15

Dan was rubbing a sore shoulder as they stumbled through the interior of the church.

"Still hurts, huh?" whispered Amy.

"Falling out of a helicopter and being crushed by your big sister will do that to a guy. I'm just glad I didn't land on my head."

"That makes two of us. Next time, think twice before pressing the red button."

"It got us out of there!" Dan protested.

Two seconds after the trapdoor in the Shark had shut, Dan had pressed a glowing red button that dropped the floor out, sending them both tumbling out onto the pavement before Irina got close enough to see them.

"Let's just find the Amber Room and get out of here as fast as we can," said Amy. "We don't want to come face-to-face with Irina again."

"Do you see anything that looks like amber?" asked Dan. There were small lights here and there, and all the colors inside the church seemed to melt into the white marble floor.

"Let's try up there," said Amy. She started walking down the middle aisle that separated the pews. It was eerie being in a church at night, especially one with a tomb underneath it, and Amy shuddered at the thought of what might jump out from the shadows. Dan thought the pews looked like rows of black teeth.

The floor was worn and grooved at the front of the church. Looking down, Dan was the first to see what they'd been looking for.

"Amber squares."

Burnt-orange tiles were beginning to appear every few feet between the marble.

"It looks like a trail of blood," said Dan.

They followed the amber tiles around the altar and down a flight of stone steps. A cold wisp of air brushed Dan's cheek as he opened the door at the bottom of the stairs and peered down a darkened passageway.

The underground hallway led twenty feet in one direction and then turned into the shadows. They walked, careful not to make any noise, until they stood at the cross of a T. The walls turned to concrete slab, and Dan had the distinct feeling they were about to enter the restricted area.

"I think we should go that way," said Amy, pointing to the left. At the end of a long hallway, a murky bulb shed light on an orange door bolted to the concrete wall with thick iron hinges. It looked like it belonged in a bank, not a church.

"Why am I so n-n-nervous?" said Amy. The orange key was shaking in her hand.

"I don't know, maybe because we're about to enter a tomb at night in a place called the Church on the Blood?"

"You're n-n-not helping," said Amy.

"Give me the key. I'll open it."

Dan inserted it into a keyhole to the left of the vault door and turned his hand. A panel slid open and revealed a set of dials. The four symbols from a deck of cards appeared randomly, and Dan quickly turned the dials to diamonds and hearts. The door clicked open.

"Here we go," said Amy, taking a deep breath as Dan pulled the heavy door forward just enough for them to sneak through. The air was cool and dank, as if they were walking on packed earth.

It was dark down there and Dan couldn't feel a light switch on the wall. He flicked on their one flashlight.

"Should we close the door behind us?" asked Amy.

"Better not. What if we get locked in? I don't want them discovering our bones in ten years." Dan's thoughts flashed back to the cave in Korea.

Cobwebs hung from a low-slung ceiling as they made their way down wide steps. When they reached the bottom, Amy lost it.

"Dan, I d-d-don't think I'm—I'm—I'm . . ."

Dan grabbed his sister's hand and pointed the light into the tomb, shooting the beam into every dark corner. It was a big space, and it was filled with dusty old coffins. On the far wall, in the deepest corner of the tomb, sat one final door.

"This place is awful," said Amy. "People were gunned down in here, killed in cold blood."

She instinctively leaned toward the door they had entered, but Dan wouldn't budge.

"Amy, we're right here. What if it leads to something about Mom and Dad? Just hold my hand and close your eyes if you have to. I'll get us there. Trust me."

Dan cracked a crooked smile, but his eyes were as nervous as Amy's.

"C'mon, Amy. A history paper is scary, but this?"

For once, Amy let her brother lead and followed his instructions without argument. She closed her eyes, shuffling past six coffins filled with brittle bones. Dan kept the flashlight beam focused on the door until he'd managed to crisscross his way around a maze of the dead.

"Hold the light," said Dan. He didn't want to let go of her hand, but he needed to turn the knob on the door. Amy reached out her hand and felt for the flashlight, keeping her eyes sealed tight.

"Don't open your eyes yet," said Dan. But Amy didn't listen. She peeked and saw that Dan had opened the lid to one of the coffins.

"Are you crazy! Close that thing right now!"

"Calm down. Nothing but bones in there."

Dan set the coffin lid down and reached for the final door.

"You can turn that off now," said Dan. "We won't be needing a flashlight in here."

Dan slowly stepped inside and found himself surrounded by soft golden light. He closed the door behind him and Amy clicked off the flashlight. It was impossible to say where the light inside the room came from, but it seemed as if its source was *everywhere*, like a thousand candles were hidden in the walls.

"The Amber Room," Amy marveled. "We made it, Dan. We're in!"

The ceiling had opened up above them and rose twenty feet in the air. Every part of the room was the deep color of burnt honey shot through with dazzling light.

"Where's the light coming from?" asked Dan. "I can't figure it out."

Amy had moved to one of the walls, touching its intricate designs. Panel after panel of glowing orange framed delicately carved amber. The superb craftsmanship must have taken years to achieve. It was like the pyramids in Egypt or the ceiling of the Sistine Chapel in Rome. Yet Dan and Amy stood within the golden light of its walls.

"Here it is," said Amy. She'd found a table made entirely of amber, upon which sat an outrageously ornate golden clock. Dan crossed through the center of the room, past a massive sculpture of a man on a horse high on a pedestal and a bank of ominous black file cabinets.

They were standing in a room almost no one had seen since before the Second World War. They'd been pushed and pulled all over Russia, but they'd prevailed. As far as the outside world was concerned, this was a priceless treasure that had long been lost forever. Dan's heart welled with pride as he looked at Amy.

"We need to turn the clock dial to midnight," said Amy. "Then one, then midnight again."

Dan crept a little closer to the clock and felt around for a dial that would allow him to change the time.

"Got it," he said, spinning the dial until the clock read midnight.

"Now forward to one o'clock," said Amy.

Dan dialed it forward, then back again to midnight, and the face of the clock came open on a single gold hinge.

Inside, Dan found a bead of amber, inscribed with the words *1 gram melted amber*.

"The clue's been right under our noses the entire time," said Amy, marveling at the bead in her hand.

"I hate it when that happens," said Dan. But he smiled at his sister. They now had five Clues and were five steps closer to claiming what Grace had called the Cahill destiny. But the Clue was not all they had come for.

Dan and Amy turned to the row of flat black file cabinets, an ominous absence of color against the softly glowing amber.

"What do we look for?" Dan asked. "Cahill? Trent? Hope and Arthur?"

"All of them. You start on that side, and I'll take the other. And hurry."

Dan opened the first drawer and rapidly flicked through the thick manila files. *Angola Mission. Arkangelsk. Assassinations.* The neatly printed labels concealed a wealth of dirty Lucian secrets.

"Dan!" called Amy, and he looked up to see Amy holding out a slim file, her face set and scared.

"Mom and Dad?" he asked.

"No," she whispered. "Madrigals."

Amy opened the file and reached for the loose papers inside. She riffled through a series of short notes handwritten in Russian. On the back, the letters had been translated into English with a ballpoint pen.

She read the first aloud:

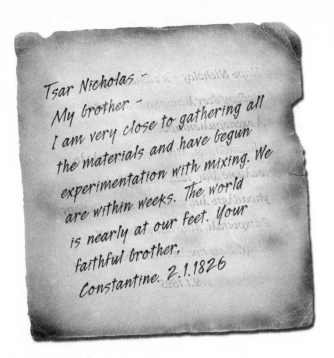

Tsar Nicholas –
My brother –
I am very close to gathering all
the materials and have begun
experimentation with mixing. We
are within weeks. The world
is nearly at our feet. Your
faithful brother,
Constantine. 2.1.1826

"Dan, this is really strange," said Amy. "I read about these two. Constantine gave up his right to the throne and let his brother Nicholas become Tsar of Russia. But this seems to indicate he did it for a purpose, so he could bring together all the clues."

"Does this mean the Lucians have all the clues?" Dan's face was pinched with anxiety. "Read the next one."

Amy set the yellowed page aside and read the words on the next piece of paper:

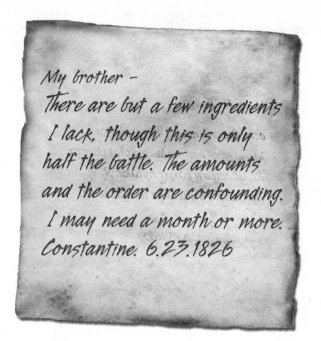

My brother —
There are but a few ingredients
I lack, though this is only
half the battle. The amounts
and the order are confounding.
I may need a month or more.
Constantine. 6.23.1826

"What if they really *do* have all the others?" asked Dan. He wasn't sure he wanted to know what was on the last slip of paper. If the Lucians really had won already, then everything he and Amy were doing was for nothing. They'd already lost.

"Oh, no," said Amy. She was scanning the last note.

"They have it, don't they? The Lucians have already finished us off."

Amy looked at her brother and then in a trembling voice read the last note:

My brother —
They found me. They have destroyed everything.
I have failed us.
Beware the Madrigals. I fear they are coming for you next.
Constantine. 10.07.1826

A heavy silence fell over the room.

"The Madrigals are more powerful than the Lucians! They maybe even had the royal family murdered!"

Amy nodded, then whispered what was on both of their minds. "And the man in black is a Madrigal."

"Let's get out of here," said Dan.

"Wait!" said Amy. "There might be something about Mom and Dad!" The kids rushed back to the files, riffling frantically until Dan found it, a thin manila folder labeled simply CAHILL, HOPE AND TRENT, ARTHUR. His heart thumped against his rib cage.

Amy looked over. "Dan! What is it?"

With trembling fingers, they opened the file

together. Inside were two Australian passports stamped CONFISCATED. Amy opened one.

"It can't be," said Dan, leaning in for a closer look.

Amy opened the second. "It's them," she said, looking at the two pictures. The names were fake, but the faces were unbearably familiar.

"Mom and Dad," said Dan. "They were here."

Amy flipped through the passport pages, crammed full with stamps from different countries. Egypt. South Africa. Nepal. Japan. Indonesia. France.

"They were searching for clues, just like us."

"Only they never finished," said Dan.

Dan's whole world narrowed to the two faces staring up at him. His mom and his dad, young and hopeful, taking on the world just as he and his sister were doing now. And failing.

Tears poured down Amy's cheeks. "It's like they've come back to help us. Almost like they're watching over us."

"They're not the only ones watching you."

Irina Spasky entered through the vault door.

"What have you done?"

Irina's voice betrayed none of the horror she felt. How could the children have been so stupid? Of all the places in the world they could have tried to break into, a Lucian black circle was the most dangerous. There was only the slimmest chance. . . .

She advanced on them quickly, crossing the room like a black cat until she had them cornered.

"Tell me what you have found. Quickly!"

"Nothing yet. We're still looking," said Dan. It was a pathetic attempt. Irina could see he held a hand behind his back and was trying to stuff something in his back pocket.

Irina surveyed the room, careful to keep them cornered.

"I see you've taken something out of its folder," she said, spotting the yellowed paper on the floor. "And you've opened the face of the clock. Clever. *Too* clever! Someone has helped you. Tell me who!"

"We didn't find anything important," said Amy. "Just some old papers."

"Give them to me at once! Your lives are in danger!"

Irina glanced toward the door. *There are minutes at best,* she thought.

But she was wrong.

"We'll take it from here."

Irina whirled around. Two men, both with veils of black over their faces, blocked the entrance to the Amber Room. In unison, they pulled back the folds of their gray jackets, revealing the Lucian crest set in a black circle.

"We are authorized by Mr. Kabra," one of them growled, holding his position at the door. "What is your clearance?"

"I created the black circle," Irina spat out. "I have the highest clearance."

The men looked at each other, sizing up the situation. Irina Spasky stared back at them, knowing what their presence meant. She had no choice now. She would have to kill the Cahill children, or these men would do it for her and kill her as well.

"I was about to clean up this situation," said Irina. "Cover the door."

The two agents retreated into the shadows, but Irina could feel their dark presence.

She hadn't thought it would come to this. *Two more minutes and I could have dealt with them, taken the secrets, and gotten them safely out.* She moved in closer, reaching behind her for the dagger concealed at her back.

The girl seemed to sense the coldness that was coming. She pressed herself in front of her brother, protectively. "We'll give you what you want," said Amy. "Just let us go. Please."

"It's too late," said Irina. "I tried."

When you lose a child, you lose your soul.

The dagger felt like ice in her hand.

There was a sharp crack from behind her. Irina turned to see shadows struggling on the wall of the darkened tomb.

"Behind you!" cried Irina.

One of the agents screamed. Irina felt a flame of wild hope and barked out to Amy and Dan, "Stay where you are!"

She crouched like a cat and burst through the doorway. Voices and shadows bounced off the wall, echoing in her brain. At first she wasn't sure, but then . . .

"You?" she gasped, her eyes latched on the wiry figure of a man dressed all in black, lunging for the Lucian agents with the blunt end of a metal pole.

Dan and Amy didn't waste any time. The second Irina entered the darkness beyond the door they followed, creeping into the tomb behind her. There was slashing and yelling and the sound of someone hitting the ground, and Dan's and Amy's shocked eyes made out the outline of a man in black locked in struggle with Irina Spasky.

Dan crept low along the first coffin, raised its lid as quietly as he could, and slid inside. Amy hesitated, but Dan took hold of her hand and wouldn't let go. She climbed in and Dan pulled the lid of the coffin shut. They listened as combatants crashed against walls and howled in pain, one of them falling against the very coffin in which they hid.

"They've escaped!" cried one of the Lucian agents.

"We have?" whispered Dan.

"I see them!"

The gravelly voice was one they hadn't heard before; it was followed by the sound of someone running from the tomb and back into the church.

"That had to be the man in black," whispered Amy. "Is he *helping* us?"

"No way," whispered Dan. He paused until it was silent, then he lifted the coffin lid ever so slightly and peered out into the darkness.

Everyone was gone.

Dan carefully lowered the lid and he and Amy waited, quiet as mice, in a coffin filled with the bones of the royal dead.

CHAPTER 16

Two hours later, Dan and Amy received a call on Nellie's phone in the coffin. The phone vibrated in Amy's pocket, shocking her out of her half slumber. Dan had fallen asleep, unmoved by the glowing green light as Amy held the phone to her eyes.

Unidentified caller. Perfect.

She decided to risk a whisper.

"Hello?"

The line was barely working underground, and Amy strained to hear the scarcely discernible, static-filled voice on the other end. All Amy could make out was the word *safe*, which she took to mean the coast was clear. It was a female voice, so it was probably Nataliya. *Or Irina trying to smoke us out.* She pushed the thought aside.

Amy nudged Dan hard enough to wake him and he grumbled, trying to nestle in. The bones beneath them sounded hollow and dry.

"I just got a call. Someone said it's safe."

THE 39 CLUES

166

"You don't have to tell me twice," said Dan, pushing up on the coffin lid without another word of encouragement.

They both peered into the darkness. The doors had been closed. There was no light at all.

"Here goes," said Amy.

She turned on the flashlight and they were blinded by the harsh light of the beam. Amy sent the light dancing from wall to wall, coffin to coffin, until it rested on the door that would lead them out of the tomb and into the church upstairs.

They got out as quietly as they could, though to Amy's horror, she heard the sound of bones breaking under her weight.

"Probably just ribs," said Dan. "It's not like he's using them for anything. Who called?"

"I'm not sure. I think it was Nataliya."

They arrived at the exit. The card deck symbols did not appear from the tomb side of the door. It simply opened, and they were free.

The next morning, ensconced in a Yekaterinburg hotel with Nellie on her way, Dan made a phone call.

"You're not driving a monster truck, are you?" Dan asked Hamilton Holt.

"Not yet, but the day is young."

"Got your clue. Are you ready?"

"I've been ready for two days. Lay it on me."

"One gram melted amber."

"Dude, that's gross. Who's Amber?"

Dan laughed. He could imagine Hamilton Holt grinning on the other side of the line.

Eisenhower grabbed the phone and yelled into it.

"Don't think this means anything. We're done partnering! Siberia and back was a raw deal and you know it. You used us!"

"Okay, Mr. Holt, whatever you say. Game on."

"Game on!" Amy agreed.

To: All Lucians
From: Vikram Kabra
Re: New strategy

My esteemed fellow Lucians,
The hunt for the 39 Clues has proved more complicated than expected.
It's time to make the other Cahill branches feel the full force of Lucian
power, even if it gets a little ... messy. I am sending all agents into the
field to join the hunt, and I authorize you to use whatever means
necessary to find the Clues. Any "accidents" involving rival Cahills
will be overlooked. Just get the job done.

Vikram Kabra

— Vikram Kabra

HOW TO START

1. Go to www.the39clues.com
2. Click on "JOIN NOW" and choose a username and password.
3. Explore the Cahill world and track down Clues.

There are over $100,000 in prizes for lucky Clue hunters.

Read the Books. Collect the Cards. Play the Game. Win the Prizes

DEC 0 9 2009

COME ALONE,
AS YOUR PARENTS DID,
OR DON'T COME AT ALL.
-NRR